"My lipstick is all gone.

"What?"

"Kissing will mak

that?"

"I..."

Lacey caught the front of Gabe's sweatshirt and pulled him forward, planting a kiss smack on his lips. For a moment he was caught off guard, but found himself responding.

Pulling back, she licked her lips. "Cool and chocolaty. Nice." She puckered up. "Are they pink?"

He cracked a smile. He couldn't help himself. She was infectious and tempting and drawing him into her delightful personality.

"You are crazy."

"See?" She touched his lips with one finger, and he wanted to grab it with his teeth and nibble and... "I made you smile. It helps to be a little crazy and not take life so seriously."

Dear Reader,

Welcome back to Horseshoe, Texas (*The Sheriff of Horseshoe, Texas*, Harlequin American Romance, March 2009; *One Night in Texas*, Harlequin American Romance, May 2014). This is a story about learning to love and live again. I have to warn you—there are some scenes that are sad, but if you hang in there, you'll cheer for Lacey and Gabe and maybe even shed a few tears of joy for them.

This story came out of nowhere. Late one night I was watching reruns of *Everybody Loves Raymond*. Ray wanted to tell Ally the truth about Santa Claus. Debra was adamantly against it. Back and forth it went with their crazy antics. Then I read a story on the internet about a woman who had lost her husband and wanted to make Christmas special for her little girl. But all the little girl wanted was for her daddy to come home. These two things got me thinking. What would you do if someone told your child there was no Santa Claus? No Christmas? And what if you had to handle it alone while dealing with a heartbreaking loss?

We've all lost loved ones and know how difficult it is to let go. Lacey has lost her father and has guardianship of her six-year-old half sister, Emma. Her next-door neighbor, Gabe Garrison, has lost his eight-year-old son in an accident. This was a difficult story to write because of the grief, but a dog named Pepper and a little girl who doesn't believe in Christmas anymore pulls it all together in an unimaginable way. Keep reading to the very last page and you'll believe in miracles, too.

Merry Christmas!

With love and thanks,

Linda Warren

You can email me at Lw1508@aol.com, or send me a message on Facebook, www.facebook.com/lindawarrenauthor, or Twitter @texauthor, or write me at P.O. Box 5182, Bryan, TX 77805. Visit my website at www.lindawarren.net. Your mail and thoughts are deeply appreciated.

A TEXAS HOLIDAY MIRACLE

—

LINDA WARREN

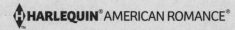

HARLEQUIN® AMERICAN ROMANCE®

Recycling programs
for this product may
not exist in your area.

ISBN-13: 978-0-373-75547-9

A Texas Holiday Miracle

Printed in U.S.A.

ABOUT THE AUTHOR

Two-time RITA® Award-nominated and award-winning author Linda Warren loves her job, writing happily-ever-after books for Harlequin. Drawing upon her years of growing up on a farm/ranch in Texas, she writes about sexy heroes, feisty heroines and broken families with an emotional punch, all set against the backdrop of Texas. Her favorite pastime is sitting on her patio with her husband watching the wildlife, especially the injured ones that are coming in pairs these days: two Canada geese with broken wings, two does with broken legs and a bobcat ready to pounce on anything tasty. Learn more about Linda and her books at her website, www.lindawarren.net, or on Facebook, www.facebook.com/authorlindawarren.

Books by Linda Warren

HARLEQUIN AMERICAN ROMANCE

THE CHRISTMAS CRADLE
CHRISTMAS, TEXAS STYLE: "MERRY TEXMAS"
THE COWBOY'S RETURN
ONCE A COWBOY
TEXAS HEIR
THE SHERIFF OF HORSESHOE, TEXAS
HER CHRISTMAS HERO
TOMAS: COWBOY HOMECOMING
ONE NIGHT IN TEXAS

Visit www.lindawarren.net for more titles.

A special thanks to my go-to ladies, Cindi, Joan, Charissa and Tammy, who know everything from kids to Christmas to plotting. Thank you!

Dedication

I dedicate this book to the readers, who write to me, buy my books, come to book signings, encourage me and support me. Your friendship means the world to me. Wishing you love, joy and happiness this holiday season.
And a miracle or two. Love, Linda

Chapter One

Christmas was the happiest time of the year for many people, but for Lacey Carroll it would be the saddest. Too much had happened to…

The front door slammed with the strength of a gale-force wind. She paused in spooning macaroni and cheese onto a plate. Not another bad day. This would make four in a row. She placed the pot on the stove, wiped her hands on a Frosty the Snowman dish towel and made her way into the living room.

Her six-year-old half sister, Emma, sat in the middle of the sofa with her arms clutched across her chest, her face scrunched into a dipped-in-vinegar frown. One of her pigtails had come undone and stuck out in a snarl on the left side of her head. Grass and bits of leaves were tangled in her blond hair. Smears of dirt marred her face, her red T-shirt and her jeans. Her sneakers were filthy, the shoelaces undone. She'd been fighting. Again!

Before their father, Jack, had passed away five months ago, he'd asked Lacey to care for Emma, so Lacey was now Emma's legal guardian. She couldn't refuse her father's dying wish, even though she had a good job in Austin and her own life. At twenty-eight, she'd made a life-changing decision because she loved her sister.

Days like this, though, tried her patience and reminded her how ill equipped she was to raise a child.

She'd bought child-rearing books and kept a mental one filled with common sense in her head. On most days she needed both.

"What happened?" Lacey asked in her best authoritative voice.

"Don't talk to me. I'm mad," Emma shot back.

"Lose the attitude. What happened?"

Emma glared at her through narrowed eyes. "I told you don't talk to me."

"And I told you to lose the attitude. Now!"

Emma turned her face away in anger.

Lacey sat beside her. "What happened?" she asked again, this time in a more soothing tone.

Emma whipped her head around. "I wanted to hit him in his big fat nose."

Oh, good heavens. Lacey took a deep breath. "Who did you want to hit in the nose? You know hitting is against our rules. Daddy's rules."

"Brad Wilson. Daddy would've hit him, too."

"I don't think so. Daddy didn't believe in violence."

Emma's face crumpled. "He said…said…there's no Santa Claus, and Jimmy and I…were big babies for believing in him."

Oh, no! Lacey flipped through pages of the mental book in her head. She knew what Emma's next question was going to be and she had to have an answer. A good one.

"Is it true, Lacey? Is there no Santa? Did Daddy put my gifts under the tree?" Big green eyes, just like Lacey's, begged for an answer.

As Lacey saw it, she had three options. Lie like she'd never lied before. Tell Emma Brad was teasing her. Or offer the truth. How could she tell a six-year-old there was no Santa Claus?

Her father had told Lacey he wanted her always to be honest with Emma just as he'd been honest with Lacey. Still…

She searched for the right thing to say. Lie, lie, lie, her inner voice kept chanting. If she did, Emma would find out soon enough. But she'd still have time to believe like a little girl should.

Lacey scooted closer and wrapped an arm around Emma. "You know there's more to Christmas than Santa Claus and receiving gifts."

"No, there isn't. Christmas is about getting gifts from Santa Claus."

Lacey prayed for patience…and wisdom. "Christmas is about the birth of Jesus Christ, and we celebrate his life by giving gifts. Sometimes giving is better than receiving."

"No, it isn't. Without Santa Claus there is no Christmas." Emma's eyes widened in realization. "There is no Santa Claus. No!" She fell sideways on the sofa and howled as if the world had come to an end.

Lacey gave her a minute and frantically breezed through the book in her head, but the pages were blank. Maybe mothers who had given birth had all the parenting answers. Lacey didn't have a clue how to soothe a little girl's broken heart, except to love her. She gathered a wailing Emma into her arms. Hitting Brad in the nose didn't seem like a bad idea at the moment.

"Shh." Lacey stroked Emma's hair, picking out bits of grass and leaves. "We'll still have Christmas. When you wake up Christmas morning, all your gifts will be under the tree and we'll have hot chocolate and cookies like always. Nothing has changed."

"It has, too." Emma sniffled into Lacey's chest. "I don't want any gifts if they don't come from Santa Claus."

"Not even that red bicycle you've been wanting?"

Emma thought for a second. "No. I don't want nothin'."

Lacey cradled her sister close. "Sweetie, Christmas is a feeling that you have in here." She placed her hand on Emma's chest. "It makes you feel good to believe in an imaginary figure who will grant your every wish. It's every child's dream. But in reality it's those people around us who love us and give us that feeling and make us feel joy and love." She poked Emma in the chest again. "All you have to do is believe in Santa, and he's right there, just like Jesus Christ. You learned that in church. As long as you believe, no one can take that feeling from you. It's warm and comforting and brings unimaginable joy. You'll feel it's Christmas because I love you and I will make Christmas as special as I can."

"But you're not Santa."

"I am Santa." She tickled Emma's rib cage. "Don't you feel all warm and fuzzy inside?"

Emma giggled. "You're weird, Lacey."

"But you love me."

Emma snuggled closer. "Uh-huh."

Lacey sagged with relief. Maybe they could get through this.

The doorbell rang and Emma rose. "I'll get it."

"No. You go brush the trash out of your hair and I'll get the door."

"Aw, Lacey."

Lacey pointed toward the hall. "Go." Emma dragged her feet toward her bedroom and Lacey went to answer the door. Sharon Wilson and her two sons stood there.

Emma came racing back, her fist raised in the air. "I'm gonna hit him in his big fat nose."

Lacey caught her before she could accomplish her goal. "Stop it."

Sharon and her boys took a step backward. "She is a little aggressive, Lacey."

Lacey bristled. "Your son just ruined her Christmas, so I'd be careful what you say."

"I'm sorry, Lacey. My husband will handle this when he comes home."

"I'm not sure what your husband can do. The damage is already done, and I'm not happy about it. Your son was very cruel to ruin their Christmas."

"They're stupid kids, and…"

Sharon popped Brad on the back of the head with her hand. "Shut up. Your father will deal with you when he gets home. Go to the house and wait for me." Brad ran away, but Jimmy waved shyly at Emma before following.

"Could we talk for a minute?" Sharon asked.

Lacey nudged Emma toward the hall. "Go brush your hair." Surprisingly, she went.

Sharon twisted her hands. "I know Emma's been through a rough time and I understand that, but I feel it's best if our kids don't play together anymore."

You hussy almost erupted from Lacey's mouth. The woman had nerve. Lacey quickly calmed her rising temper. Jimmy was Emma's only playmate, and her sister needed a friend. Since their father's death, Emma had alienated everyone around her. Lacey was working to change that, but days like this didn't help.

Lacey swallowed her pride. "Emma and Jimmy play well together. It's your older son who's causing all the problems."

"I know. Since he turned ten, I can't handle him anymore. I leave that up to my husband. I'm really sorry, Lacey. Jimmy likes Emma."

"Can Jimmy come here to play with Emma, because I really don't want Emma around Brad?"

"Well, I guess that would be okay." Sharon looked toward her house down the street. "I better go before the boys get into another fight. Again, I'm sorry."

Lacey closed the door and made her way to the kitchen. Emma bounded in with her hair all around her face and climbed onto a bar stool.

"Did you wash your hands?"

"Yes."

"We'll have to wash your hair tonight."

Emma brushed it from her face. "Why?"

"Because it's dirty."

"Lacey, you always make me do things I don't want to."

"That's life, snuggle bunny." Lacey placed a plate in front of Emma and sat beside her on the other bar stool.

Emma stared at the food. "What's this?"

"Supper. Your favorite mac and cheese out of a box. Green beans, turkey and cranberry sauce left over from Thanksgiving."

"But you burned it."

"I cut the burned part off and the turkey is still good. Eat it."

"You're gonna kill us, Lacey. You're not supposed to eat burned food."

"Eat and stop complaining."

Emma ate the mac and cheese, most of the turkey and picked at the green beans. Lacey had to admit she was a lousy cook. Her mother was, too. Her dad had been in charge in the kitchen. It shouldn't be that hard, but she seemed to burn everything she made. In Austin, she ate out mostly because she was so busy. But a child needed a healthy diet.

"These beans are yucky. You're supposed to put butter on them or something. Daddy did."

Butter. Why hadn't she thought of that? She had to buy a cookbook or something. Eating at the local diner was getting old. She'd attempted Thanksgiving dinner because she wanted it to be special for Emma, but she wasn't fooling anyone. It had been a disaster. And kind of lonely with just the two of them.

She carried her plate to the sink. "If you're finished, go take your bath and I'll do the dishes. I'll be in to help with your hair."

Emma climbed off the stool and dashed down the hall. After putting the dishes in the dishwasher, Lacey wiped the counter. A banging sounded from next door. Their neighbor, Gabe Garrison, was working on something. He always was.

Lacey had never actually had a conversation with the man. Her father had introduced them months earlier and Gabe had said hello and walked away. Her dad had explained that the man's son had been killed in an ATV accident—an ATV that Gabe had bought the child for his birthday.

According to her father, Gabe had been a lawyer in Austin. After the accident, he'd tried to continue working, but hadn't been able to. He and his wife had divorced and he'd moved back to Horseshoe, where he'd been raised, to grieve alone. He wanted privacy and Lacey understood that, but that was hard to explain to a six-year-old.

Gabe's son's dog, Pepper, was in the backyard and a big temptation for Emma. Lacey lost track of the number of times she'd told Emma not to go into Gabe's yard.

Emma never listened. If she heard the dog, she went over, and then Lacey would get a short lecture from Gabe on respecting a man's privacy.

Leaning against the counter, Lacey wondered what her friends in Austin were doing. Probably getting ready to go out for the night to a club to party. That had been Lacey's old life, and she missed it in ways that were hard to explain. Maybe because that life had been care-free with very little responsibility. Now responsibility weighed on her like an anvil around her neck. Some days it was hard to stand upright for the weight. She didn't re-gret her decision to raise Emma. She just regretted she wasn't more experienced at being responsible.

Her parents had divorced after nineteen years of mar-riage, and Lacey's young life had been thrown into tur-moil. Her college dream had been forgotten because there was no money to send her, so she worked at Macy's in the makeup department. Her mother worked there, too. It hadn't been ideal, but it had been a job.

A short three months later, her mother had remarried and Lacey had moved out of the house and been on her own. She'd gotten a job with a party-planning company. She'd loved it, and she'd been away from the influence of her mother and her mother's new husband.

Her dad had moved back to Horseshoe, where he had grown up. A year later he'd married Mona and they'd had Emma. Her father had been happier than Lacey had ever seen him. She'd continued to visit, much to her mother's displeasure, and had enjoyed spending time with them. Never in a million years had she imagined her dad's and Mona's lives would be cut so short.

She tucked the memories away and hurried to help her sister. Bathed and in her jammies, Emma carried her soft blanket, her Pooh bear and a pillow to watch TV.

"I'll see if I can find a Christmas show." Lacey flipped through the channels.

"I don't want to watch a Christmas show. There is no Christmas."

Lacey let that pass, hoping Emma's attitude would change. At six, it changed often. Sometimes faster than Lacey could keep up. "*Shrek the Halls* is on. You like Shrek."

Emma curled up with the blanket on the sofa and watched without complaining. Score one for Lacey. "I have to get clothes out of the dryer, but I'll be right back to watch it with you."

"'Kay."

Lacey folded the laundry and put it away. She thought of taking a shower, but decided to wait until Emma had gone to bed. Her sister needed all of Lacey's attention. She stopped short in the living room doorway. The blanket, Pooh Bear and pillow were on the sofa, but Emma was not.

"No! No! No!" Lacey ran for the back door. The only place Emma would go was to see Pepper, and Lacey did not want another confrontation with Gabe the Grouch.

Her father had installed a privacy fence around their backyard. A gate opened into Gabe's yard. Lacey rushed through it and stopped suddenly. Gabe stood there with a scowl as big as Texas on his face.

The man was tall, six foot or more. He wore jeans and a dark flannel shirt. He looked foreboding. A chill slid through her that had nothing to do with the temperature. His hair was long and his face unshaven, as if he didn't care, which Lacey knew he didn't. His jeans and shirt seemed to hang on his thin body. He probably ate very little, but he still was a very handsome man in roguish sort of way.

"Would you please keep your sister out of my yard?" The words were cold and sharp, just as he'd intended, she was sure.

She stepped around his dark presence and went to Emma, who was kneeling by Pepper. The black lab was lying in a dog bed and Emma was stroking her.

She reached for Emma's arm. "Let's go. You're not supposed to be here."

Emma looked at her with beseeching eyes. "But Pepper wants me here."

The dog whimpered as if it were in pain. Was the dog sick? It was none of her business, she had to remind herself. She tugged on Emma's arm and half dragged her back toward the gate.

It was a chilly winter night and Emma just had on her PJs. "Run to the house. I'll be right there."

Emma glanced at Gabe and then raced for the back door.

Lacey faced the dark knight, not sure what to say, but she knew she had to say something.

Gabe didn't give her time to voice her feelings. "If she comes into my yard one more time, I'm nailing the gate shut."

Lacey looked into his eyes. If she had never known or felt pain, she would know what it was by that one glance. The crevices around his eyes were permanently etched in place as if forged by fire. His eyes were hollow, dark pits, and the only emotion he showed was the anger that flared from their depths. Normally, when she saw all the angst on his face, her retorts died on her lips. The man had been hurt enough. But today she didn't back down.

"That gate is half mine, and if you nail it shut, I will un-nail it." She was ready for battle, but then he did his usual thing. He turned and walked away.

Chapter Two

Gabe tuned out the woman. He had no desire to talk to her or anyone. He didn't understand why she couldn't respect his privacy. When Jack was alive, Gabe had had no problems. Now the kid was out of control and the woman had no idea how to handle her. Both of them had tried his patience for the last time. He would nail the gate shut without a second thought.

He opened the back door and then picked up Pepper, bed and all, and carried her inside. She was getting too weak to walk. As he placed her by the sofa he noticed she was trembling in pain. Gritting his teeth, he knew he had to give her another shot. He went into the kitchen and got the medication the vet had given him. After giving her an injection, he stroked her until she drifted into sleep.

Sinking back onto the sofa, he drew a long breath. The vet had said it was time to put Pepper down. She was in too much pain from cancer, but she had been Zack's dog and he couldn't bring himself to do it. He looked at all the pictures of Zack he had hung on the walls. His son was in this room. He was everywhere. And Gabe had to take care of the dog his son had loved.

He rested his head on the back of the sofa and closed his eyes. The moment he did he saw his laughing, happy son and pain pierced his heart. Pain was all he felt these days. Life meant nothing to him. He couldn't understand how fate could be so cruel as to take a child from his parents. Gabe didn't know right from wrong anymore, and it didn't matter. All that mattered was that he remembered his son every moment of every day.

That was the only thing that kept him going.

THE NEXT MORNING Lacey let Emma sleep in. Last night, they hadn't talked because Lacey was too upset. She had scolded Emma and put her to bed early.

Lacey was making breakfast when Emma trudged in and climbed onto the bar stool. Smoke spiraled from the toaster and the alarm went off, shrilling loud enough to wake the neighborhood.

"Not again." Emma buried her face in her hands.

Lacey pulled off her sneaker and threw it at the smoke alarm. The device flew off and landed in the kitchen sink, causing the deafening sound to stop. The blackened toast popped up at the same time.

Emma looked through her fingers. "You're gonna kill us, Lacey."

She opened the window to let the smoke out. "I have everything under control," she said, hoping she sounded convincing. Inside, she was shaking and wondering how a twenty-eight-year-old woman could be so hopeless in the kitchen.

She threw the burned slices of bread in the garbage and put four more in the toaster. Stupid smoke alarm wasn't stopping her.

"You have to know when to push up the lever," Emma told her. "Daddy knew."

Next trip to town Lacey was buying a new toaster. She was tired of fooling with this relic. While she watched the bread, she slipped her sneaker back on. Just as the slices were starting to burn, she pushed up the lever, and then buttered the toast, added grape jelly and placed it on the plate with the scrambled eggs.

"Breakfast," she said, sliding it in front of Emma with a smile.

Emma rolled her eyes. "Now we don't have a smoke alarm."

"I'll get the ladder and put it back after breakfast. Nothing I can't handle."

Emma ate her breakfast and Lacey munched on a piece of toast. Nothing like starting the day with a little excitement. She hoped Gabe hadn't heard the alarm. She had a feeling he didn't hear much of anything besides the demons in his head.

Brushing hair from her face, Emma asked, "Are you mad at me?"

Lacey knew Emma was talking about last night. "You disobeyed me."

Emma swallowed a mouthful of egg. "Mr. Gabe doesn't mean it when he says for me not to come into his yard."

"Emma, sweetie, yes, he does."

"But I hear Pepper and I have to go."

Lacey sighed. "Pepper is not our dog, and we have to respect Mr. Gabe's privacy. Do you understand that?"

Emma shook her head.

Lacey was all out of options. She'd just have to watch Emma more closely. She clapped her hands to brighten the moment. "Today we get the Christmas tree. Daddy always got it the Saturday after Thanksgiving."

"There's no Santa Claus, Lacey!" Emma shouted. "We don't need a Christmas tree!"

"Well, I still believe in Christmas, and I'm putting up a tree right in front of the windows in the living room."

"I'm not looking at it." Emma jumped off the bar stool.

"You don't have to." It broke Lacey's heart that Emma was being so adamant about this. Maybe if she kept pushing, Emma would start to believe again. There was no Christmas without the magic of belief. Somehow, Lacey had to find a way to put a little more of that good stuff in their lives. "Go get dressed while I put our dishes in the dishwasher."

Lacey managed to reattach the smoke alarm. The green light came on, so she felt sure it was working and ready for the next round.

THE CHRISTMAS TREE lot was off the square in Horseshoe. People were out and about searching for the perfect tree.

"I'm not looking," Emma told her.

Lacey didn't say anything. She got out of the car and walked around, inspecting the trees. Soon Emma was right beside her. It was taking a while, but Lacey was learning parenting tricks.

She picked out a seven-foot Douglas fir and had the man put a stand on it. Then he tied it on to the top of her SUV.

While they were waiting, a little girl came over and said something to Emma. To Lacey's shock, Emma frowned and kicked at her with her sneaker. The little girl ran back to her father, who was measuring a tree.

This wasn't the place to discipline Emma. She'd wait until they got home. Lacey didn't know if she had the strength or the capabilities to continue to deal with this kind of behavior. But she would keep trying.

As they pulled into their driveway, Lacey saw Gabe in his front yard digging up a shrub that had died. The black knit cap he wore on his head gave him a dangerous, fierce look. He didn't even raise his head as they got out. He just kept digging.

Before Lacey could stop her, Emma darted over to Gabe. Lacey wanted to pull out her hair. This was turning out to be the worst day ever. She ran behind Emma and caught her just before she reached the man.

"Whatcha doing?" Emma asked.

Lacey took her hand and led her back toward their house without saying a word to the man who was glaring at them.

"You disobeyed me again. Go into the house and sit on the sofa until I get there. And do not turn on the TV. Do you understand me?"

Emma nodded and stomped toward the front door. Lacey unlocked it and Emma went inside. First, Lacey had to get the tree off the SUV, and then she would deal with her sister.

She grabbed a pair of scissors and the kitchen stool. She cut the strings off the tree and tried to lift it from the SUV, but soon found she couldn't. The stool gave her some height, but not enough for her to hoist the heavy tree. The branches scratched her face and she said a cuss word under her breath. How was she going to get the tree off the car?

GABE KEPT DIGGING, trying to ignore the crazy lady on the rickety kitchen stool. She was going to fall and break her neck, but it was none of his concern. She stood on tiptoes and tried to heave it off, but to no avail. The woman was a menace. Her smoke alarm went off regularly. He'd heard it that morning. Evidently, she couldn't cook. The stool wobbled and she grabbed the car to keep from falling.

Do not help. Do not help.

The warning in his head was clear, and he always obeyed it because he didn't want to interact with anyone. But even he had a breaking point. He propped the shovel against the house and walked over.

With one gloved hand he gripped the tree trunk and lifted it from the SUV.

"Oh…oh…" she stammered, almost falling off the stool again.

"Where do you want this?" he snapped.

"Uh…" She climbed off the stool and headed for the front door. "In here."

Inside the house she pointed to the living room windows. He placed the tree in the spot.

"Hi, Mr. Gabe," the little girl said from the sofa.

He didn't want to engage in conversation, so he left. On his way back to his house, he cursed himself. He didn't want to get involved, and helping the crazy lady was a sure way for that to happen. He was trying desperately to keep his privacy, and he'd probably just made a big mistake.

That suffocating feeling came over him, and he went into the house to check on Pepper. She was better this morning and had even trotted outside to do her business. The shots always helped for a while. How he wished they could last longer. Soon he'd have to make a decision, and it was tearing him up inside. He just couldn't let go.

He wasn't sure what he was afraid of. The vet had said it was the best thing for the dog, but how could killing something be good? If he did what the vet had suggested, it would be like letting go of Zack all over again.

Some things were just too painful to endure twice.

LACEY WAS STUNNED. The Grouch had helped. She was still trying to digest that. Maybe things would change.

Maybe he would be friendlier. And maybe she would sprout wings and fly. Oh, yeah. Gabe Garrison had not changed. She had no idea why he had helped, and he probably had none, either.

She had other important matters to take care of. For the first time, she'd become aware of how Emma brightened when Gabe was around. She'd formed a connection with him and Pepper.

Their father had raised Emma. Mona had died six months after Emma's birth. While Mona had been pregnant, the doctors had discovered cancer. Mona had refused any treatment until after the baby was born, but by then the aggressive cancer had spread. She hadn't lasted long.

Emma was more comfortable around men, and she'd somehow transferred that need for a father figure to Gabe. That was why Emma kept saying Gabe didn't mean what he said. *Another problem.* Lacey had too many to deal with. She'd tackle the most pressing first.

"Mr. Gabe brought our tree in," Emma said, her eyes bright. It didn't escape Lacey that Emma had said *our.* Maybe Lacey was winning her over.

She knelt in front of Emma, who sat on the sofa. "Why did you disobey me again? You're not supposed to go into Gabe's yard."

Emma twisted her hands. "I forgot and I wanted to see what he was doing."

"Emma…"

"Really. I forgot."

Lacey had a feeling she was fighting a losing battle about Gabe and his privacy, so she decided to tackle another problem. "What did the little girl at the tree lot say to you?"

Emma looked down at her hands. "She said hi."

"Then why did you kick at her?"

"'Cause I don't like her."

"Why? She seemed real nice and she was there with her daddy...." Lacey's voice trailed off as something occurred to her. "You don't like her because she has a daddy and you don't."

From the shattered look in Emma's eyes, Lacey knew she was right. She wanted to stand up and do a jig. She'd gotten it right. Maybe parenting didn't come through the birth canal. Maybe it was trial and error.

She sat next to Emma. "You have a father, and he loved you more than life itself. You do know that, don't you?"

"But he's not here." The little voice wavered. "Why did my daddy have to go?"

Lacey gathered her into her arms. "I don't know, sweetie. I wish I had an answer that would make you feel better, but I don't. Sometimes bad things happen in life, and we have to adjust and go on. That's what Daddy wanted for you, and you promised him you wouldn't be sad."

"I miss Daddy," Emma cried.

"I do, too." Lacey held her sister and hoped by talking she could ease some of her pain. "Close your eyes."

"Why?"

"Just do it."

Emma scrunched her eyes together.

"Now, can you see Daddy? Try to see him."

"I can. I can see Daddy."

Lacey held her tighter. "Is he smiling?"

"Yes. He's smiling at me." Emma's voice grew excited.

"When you're feeling lonely and when you think other children have a daddy and you don't, just close your eyes and your daddy is right there. Always. And I'm right here. Always."

Emma leaned away. "Are you mad at me?" It was Emma's stock question when she'd done something wrong.

Lacey kissed her forehead. "No, sweetie. I'm not mad at you. But the next time that little girl says hi to you, I want you to say hi back. I do not want you kicking at anyone. Understand?"

Emma nodded.

"I'll call Sharon and see if Jimmy can come over and play for a while."

Emma jumped up. "Oh, boy! I'll get my Legos out."

And just like that the morning turned around. For the time being.

Jimmy came over. Lacey made them peanut-butter-and-jelly sandwiches for lunch, and then they returned to building stuff in the living room. As Lacey wiped the counter, she heard banging. And it was close. He wouldn't!

She ran outside and pushed on the gate, but it wouldn't budge. She used her body and shoved with all her might, and still the gate wouldn't move. Damn him! She wasn't going to let Gabe get away with this.

Back in the house, she hollered to the kids, "I'm going outside."

"'Kay," Emma shouted back.

Lacey went into the garage and found a hammer. Then she grabbed the kitchen stool that was still by the car and marched around to the fence between Gabe's and their house. She stepped up on the ladder and then vaulted over. Misjudging the height, she landed on her butt. She was winded for a moment, but she still had the hammer in her hand.

Getting to her feet, she took a long breath and marched

to the gate. A large board was nailed across it. She tried to pry it away with the hammer, but she wasn't strong enough. Damn! She kicked at the gate. Frustrated, she sank to the ground with her back against it.

"What are you doing?"

She looked up into the brooding eyes of the dark knight. Every time she looked at his sad face, she wanted to apologize or try to make him feel better, like she did Emma. But sometimes there was no way to make things better.

She staggered to her feet. "I was trying to pry the board away, but you nailed it securely. I hope you're happy."

Gabe just stared at her, his dark eyes orbs of never-ending sadness.

"She's a little girl and she doesn't understand. And I don't understand how you can be so cruel. How would you feel if someone had done this to your son?"

He turned as white as the fluffy clouds over his head, and Lacey thought he was going to pass out. Still, she wasn't in a relenting mood.

"If it makes you happy to keep the gate closed and us out, then by all means leave it nailed up. One day you're going to have to face the outside world and maybe even have to explain how you could hurt a six-year-old child. Your son would be so disappointed in you. Emma's made a connection to you and Pepper, but I will do my damnedest to keep her away. So be happy, Mr. Gabe Garrison. You just secured your privacy."

After saying that, she marched back to the fence and realized there was no way to get over it without the stool, which was on the other side.

Not willing to lose face, she stormed around his house and to the double gates on the other side. Stomping across his front yard, she realized she still had the hammer in her hand. What had she done? She'd traumatized a man who was barely hanging on emotionally.

Placing the hammer back in her father's toolbox, she knew she had to apologize. Later, though, when she wasn't fuming.

Gabe was so locked within himself he probably hadn't even heard what she'd said. She'd take time to cool off and then she would try to make amends. If that was possible.

She was so tired of dealing with grief and pain that she wanted to scream. There had to be a glimmer of happiness somewhere, and she intended to find it for Emma. And for herself.

But for Gabe, happiness was in his rearview mirror. And the road ahead was strewn with heartache and pain. Hope was something he didn't even want or desire. Inside, he was already as dead as his son.

Chapter Three

Gabe walked into his house and sat at the kitchen table, Pepper curled at his feet. The woman had some nerve. She didn't even know Zack or him. He looked up to stare at a photo of his son.

How would you feel if someone had done this to your child?

Don't think.

But his feelings bubbled to the surface. He would be as mad as hell. He ran his hands over his face and a tortured sigh escaped. He would have protected his son with his dying breath, except that when his son had needed him the most, Gabe hadn't been there. He'd failed his son. He'd failed to teach him how important it was to follow rules. He'd failed to discipline him. That was all on Gabe's shoulders. Gabe was the reason Zack was dead.

Another tortured sigh erupted from his throat.

Pepper whined and Gabe reached down to pat her. As he did, he saw his reflection in the glass on the stove. He didn't recognize himself. He touched his bearded face. When was the last time he'd shaved? Or showered? Or had gotten a haircut? He couldn't remember.

Your son would be so disappointed in you.

The woman was right. He recognized that somewhere in the frozen region of his mind. Zack wouldn't approve of him giving up and living his days in regret. But what else could he do? He had no reason to live anymore, but he didn't have the nerve to take his own life. He would never do that. It went against everything he believed in. So he continued to live in a hell of his own making.

One crazy woman was putting doubts in his head. *Ignore her,* he told himself. But he looked at the photo of his smiling son and knew he couldn't continue to live like this. Zack was gone and he couldn't hurt another child. But he could make things right.

IT TOOK LACEY about thirty minutes to calm down. Emma and Jimmy continued to play with the Legos and she made them a snack. Afterward, Emma wanted to know if they could go outside and play. Lacey hesitated, but Emma would find out soon enough about the gate. Lacey just had to be ready to explain.

She watched from the window while the kids chased each other and then played with a soccer ball, kicking it. Not once did Emma go to the gate, and Lacey was grateful for a little more time. Sharon called and Jimmy went home.

Not wanting to go to the diner again, Lacey made hot dogs and they had store-packaged pudding for dessert. She had to do better than this.

Emma took her bath and then curled up on the sofa to watch *How the Grinch Stole Christmas.*

Lacey couldn't get Gabe off her mind.

"Sweetie, I'm going outside just for a minute. I'll be right back."

"'Kay." Emma was already engrossed in the movie.

Lacey went through the garage and walked to Gabe's front door. She rang the bell and waited. After a moment, he opened it.

She could only stare. He'd shaved, and his long hair was slicked back as if he'd just gotten out of the shower. He wore jeans and a black T-shirt and his feet were bare. Raw masculinity seemed to reach out and touch her. She swallowed hard.

"Did you want something?" he asked, his voice wrapping around her in a soothing sensation.

"Um…"

He lifted a dark eyebrow, and his eyes were heated with an emotion she couldn't describe. It wasn't anger this time. Could it be regret?

"Did you want something?" he repeated.

She cleared her throat. "Yes. I want to apologize for what I said earlier. I was completely out of line mentioning your son."

He inclined his head, as if that was a response.

Taking a couple steps backward, she turned and walked to her house. She'd never met anyone like Gabe before. He used a bare minimum of words, and she found that odd for a man who was a lawyer—or who had been one.

Once in her garage, she took a couple of deep breaths before joining Emma to watch the rest of the movie. But the movie went right by her as thoughts of Gabe filled her head. He cleaned up better than anyone she'd ever known. He was handsome with a rugged, masculine appeal that made her pulse skitter with awareness.

She'd had a boyfriend in Austin, and they had been serious until her father had become ill and Lacey had started spending so much time in Horseshoe. Darin hadn't been happy that she'd taken on the responsibility of Emma, and they'd drifted apart. She hadn't heard from him in months.

Her mother also hadn't been pleased with Lacey's decision. But then she and her mother had never been really close. Her father had been the steadying force in her life as a child and as a teenager. Her mother had worked at Macy's for as far back as Lacey could remember—long hours and all holidays, leaving little time for her family.

Her parents were mismatched, and Lacey had never understood how they'd gotten together. Her mother was a social person who liked to go out after work. Her father had been a homebody who had enjoyed tinkering around the house.

Jack Carroll had been a postman, and her mother always had been on his case about drive and ambition. She'd wanted him to have a desk job. She'd wanted him to have prestige. It had all come to a head after her father had declined a desk job at the post office. Her mother had told him to get out and never come back. And he had. Then she'd blamed him for leaving. Her mother was the victim, and Lacey had grown tired of hearing that story.

But she was Lacey's mother, and Lacey loved her even though it was hard sometimes to deal with her. She had no idea how she was going to fit Christmas in with her mother, because her mother refused to be around Emma. Somehow she blamed the child for the reason Jack never came back.

Emma was sound asleep, holding her bear. Lacey wondered how anyone could blame an innocent child. And she wondered if her life would be filled with anything other than heartache. Getting up, she yawned, reached for the remote control and clicked off the TV. She lifted Emma into her arms and carried her to bed.

Tomorrow had to be a better day.

And the man next door had to be in a better mood. They'd made a start. Now Lacey waited for the next encounter.

THE NEXT MORNING Lacey was in a hurry to make the ten o'clock mass. Emma was being stubborn, not wanting to wear a dress or put a bow in her hair. But Lacey won that round. They walked through the doors of the little Catholic Church in Horseshoe just as the bell chimed.

Emma fidgeted during the service, and Lacey had to give her a couple of sharp stares to keep her still. Afterward, they came out of church to a cold winter day. In the parking lot, Lacey said hello to Angie and Hardy Hollister. She had met Angie when she'd first moved here. Angie was very nice and had wanted to help as much as she could after Jack's death. Angie's friend Peyton was the same. Hardy was the D.A., and Peyton's husband, Wyatt Carson, was the sheriff.

Emma brightened when she saw Angie and Hardy's daughter. Erin was almost twelve, but Emma considered her a friend.

Erin took Emma's hand and they ran to say hello to Erin's grandma and the Wiznowski family. They were a big family and owned the busiest place in town, the bakery. Lacey was still learning all of their names.

"Why does Emma look so sad?" Angie asked, her hand on her stomach. She was due at the end of March and she positively glowed.

"Brad Wilson told her there's no Santa Claus and now she doesn't want to have Christmas."

"How awful."

Hardy had his arm around his wife, and he rubbed her shoulder in a loving gesture. "Kids can be cruel."

Erin and Emma came running back and they said goodbye. Angie bent down to Emma. "Merry Christmas."

Emma twisted in her Mary Jane shoes and didn't respond.

Lacey took Emma's hand and they walked to the car. They went to the diner for lunch before heading home. Emma was very quiet. She probably was feeling lonely, just like Lacey was.

Emma plopped onto the sofa. "Can Jimmy come over to play?"

"No. He's gone to his grandmother's today. Change your clothes and we'll play games or something."

"No." The word was spoken in an angry tone.

Lacey gave her a minute. Then she placed her hands on her hips. "Go change your clothes. Now!"

Emma jumped up and ran to her room. Lacey groaned. Another one of those days. They were due for a good one. Soon.

After slipping into jeans and a pullover top, she went to check on Emma. The little girl was lying on her bed, reading a book. She took after her mother. Mona had been a librarian.

Lacey glanced around the lavender, white and purple room she'd helped their father decorate. Emma was not a girlie girl and had not wanted a pink room. Her father had bought all kinds of Barbies and a Barbie doll house and numerous other Barbie toys, but Emma barely touched them. She liked the outdoors and would rather play with a ball instead of a doll. But she did love stuffed animals, and they littered the comforter on her white four-poster bed.

Lacey sat beside her sister. "What are you reading?"

Emma closed *A Light in the Attic* and scooted up. "Why don't I have a grandma?"

Oh, that was the reason for the sulkiness. "You did have a grandma. Two, actually. Dad's mom's name was Martha and your mom's was Ruth. Grandma Martha died when I was fifteen. She would've loved you."

"She would?"

"You bet. She gave big hugs and made everyone feel loved. I always looked forward to staying with her during the summer."

"What about my other grandma?"

Lacey took a breath, hating to talk about so many deaths. But she had to be honest. "She died, too, sweetie. I never met her. She was a librarian like your mother."

Emma stared down at her sneakers. "Why does everybody have to die?"

Lacey frantically opened the book in her head and searched for answers. As always, none was suitable. She had to go with her gut feeling. "That's life, sweetie, and as you get older you'll understand more." That sounded lame even to her own ears. She was terrible at this. Hugging Emma, she said, "You know what? You can call me Lacey or you can call me Grandma. I can be both."

Emma giggled. With a hand over her mouth, she said, "You're weird, Lacey."

"How about if we walk to the park and play on the big slide and swing set?"

"'Kay." Emma jumped off the bed. "They have a really big slide. It makes my stomach feel funny and it's fun."

"Let's get our coats and go, then."

Emma grabbed her coat from a chair. As Lacey went to her room to get hers, the buzz of her cell phone stopped her.

"Just a minute, Emma. I have to answer my phone."

It was her mother. Lacey sank onto the bed, ready for another round of complaints. "Hi, Mom."

Her mother wasted no time getting started. "Since you couldn't spend Thanksgiving with me, I was hoping we could spend Christmas together."

Lacey closed her eyes and counted to three. "Mom, you know I can't leave Emma at Christmas."

"What about me? Your own mother? You have no time for me anymore. I don't know what Jack was thinking when he asked you to take care of that child. You're a young woman and should have your own life."

They had been through this so many times, and Lacey had grown weary of the subject. "It was my choice. Mona's sister offered to take Emma, but she has four children of her own. If Emma was taken from the home she'd shared with Dad, I knew it would be detrimental for her. I love my sister and I couldn't put her through that. I'm here and I intend to stay here. I will work something out for Christmas."

"Like what?"

"If you would just accept Emma, you could come to Horseshoe."

"I'm not stepping foot in the house your father shared with that woman."

Lacey wanted to beat her head against something. "He shared this house with his wife."

"I'll never forgive you for accepting her."

"Mom, have you been drinking or something? You're not making any sense. You're the one who told dad to leave. You're the one who remarried three months later. I don't know why you feel like the victim."

"Jack would have come back if it hadn't been for her."

"You'd married someone else. Are you forgetting that?"

"I only did it to get back at him. That's why the marriage didn't last."

"Mom, I'm not going through all this again. Mona and Emma made Dad very happy."

After a long pause, Joyce said, "Maybe I am being a

little irrational, but I loved your father and I never meant for him to stay away. It just turned out that way."

Finally, her mother was admitting the truth. "I know you loved him, but you were miserable the last years of your marriage."

"Lacey," a little voice call from the hallway. "Are we going to the park?"

"In a minute, sweetie. I'll be right there," she called back. "Mom, I really have to go."

"Am I going to see you at all this Christmas?"

"What about Mervin?" That was her mom's new boyfriend.

"He'll want to spend time with his kids, and I don't get along with them."

No surprise there. Her mother enjoyed being the center of attention. "Call me when you have a day off and I'll come for a visit."

"I work a lot during the holidays."

Same old line. Same old verse. "Please think about coming here for Christmas. Once you meet Emma, you'll love her. She had nothing to do with your marriage or your divorce. She's just an innocent little girl."

"I'll talk to you later," her mother said, and clicked off.

Lacey sat for a moment and wished her mother would come to grips with the past and her part in it. But maybe some things just were not doable. Or realistic, considering the way her mother felt.

Now Lacey had a little girl who was eager to go to the park. She reached for her jacket and hurried to the kitchen. But Emma wasn't there and she wasn't in the living room. Or anywhere in the house.

No! No! No!

Lacey ran out the back door and stopped short. The

gate was open. Gabe had removed the board? She walked slowly to the opening and could see Emma sitting on a lawn chair, huddled in her red-and-black coat. Gabe sat next to her in a black hoodie and jeans. They were staring at Pepper in her bed. Neither was speaking. There was complete silence.

What were they doing?

Gabe didn't seem upset that Emma was there. Lacey's first instinct was to go over and make Emma come back to their house. But something stopped her.

A plane flew overhead. A car honked and the wind rustled through the leaves of the tall oaks. Other than that, the two of them sat there in perfect harmony. Perfect silence. Lacey couldn't bring herself to interrupt.

Suddenly, Emma said, "Pepper is sick. When I was sick, my daddy took me to the doctor. You have to take Pepper to the doctor."

Gabe didn't answer or look at Emma. His eyes were on the dog.

"My daddy died, so he can't take me anymore. Lacey does. Daddy's in heaven and Lacey says he can see me. But I can't see him. I miss my daddy." Emma wiped at her eyes and Lacey wanted to run over, but again she didn't. "Do you miss your son?"

Lacey's heart sank at the question. She should get Emma before she caused Gabe any more pain. But for some reason she couldn't explain, she stood there, holding her breath, waiting for Gabe to answer.

Chapter Four

Gabe's throat locked tight. He couldn't push a sound through. Nor could he breathe. His body stiffened in protest, needing oxygen. Just when he thought the pain would get him, Pepper saved him. She whimpered, and the child jumped from her chair and went to the dog.

The little girl stroked Pepper and Gabe wanted to scream, *Don't touch her. She's Zack's dog. Get away from her.* But the words wouldn't come. In that moment he realized just how insane his thoughts were, and the lock on his throat lessened. He breathed in deeply, his lungs expanding from the much needed relief.

"Pepper is sick, Mr. Gabe," the kid said.

He knew that. He wanted to tell her it was none of her business and that she should go home. But once again the words wouldn't come. Maybe because Pepper had lifted her head and licked the child's hand. Pepper liked the kid. He'd never noticed that before. He hadn't noticed many things beyond the pain in his chest.

"She's shaking. I think she's cold." The kid noticed the blanket by the basket and gently tucked it around Pepper.

It was getting colder. He should take Pepper inside, but whenever he did, she whined to go out. He was just giving her a little more time.

The kid stood up. "I gotta go. Lacey's probably looking for me. She doesn't like it when I come over here. But you don't mind, do you?"

Yes, I mind. Please, just leave me alone.

"Lacey and me have the same father. We're sisters. Her mama lives in Austin and I've never met her. Do you have a sister?"

Yes. He should call Kate and let her know he was… what? Still living with the pain. She wouldn't want to hear that, so it was best to wait a little longer.

"I gotta go. Don't forget to take Pepper to the doctor. He'll make her all better. 'Bye."

Not this time.

The child ran to the gate. Gabe got up and squatted next to Pepper.

"You like the kid, don't you?"

Pepper nuzzled his hand in approval.

But she's not Zack. She's not Zack.

LACEY HURRIED INTO the house and was standing just inside the back door as Emma came through it.

"Oh," Emma said, startled.

Lacey folded her arms across her chest. "You've been over at Gabe's."

She would have to discipline Emma, even though it would hurt Lacey more than it did her sister. She'd let her disobey too many times, though. Gabe hadn't seemed to mind Emma being there, but Emma had done all of the talking. Gabe hadn't responded once. And Emma needed to know that she had to mind and respect other people's wishes.

"Uh…" Emma twisted her hands. "You were on the phone and I heard Pepper."

"You can't hear the dog from inside the house."

"Yes, I…"

"No." Lacey pointed a finger at Emma. "You've disobeyed me twice today, and now I have to punish you."

"No, Lacey, no. Don't punish me." Emma barreled into Lacey, wrapping her arms around Lacey's waist, and burying her face in Lacey's stomach. "I'm sorry. I won't do it again."

Lacey swallowed, trying to be strong. "You say that all the time and you still disobey me. Go to your room and sit in the time-out chair."

"No. I don't want to."

Lacey pointed toward the hall. "Go."

"No. I'll be good!" Emma wailed.

Lacey took Emma's hand and led her down the hall to her bedroom. Emma sobbed loudly the whole time and Lacey's strength waned. She pulled out Emma's desk chair and placed it in a corner.

"Take off your coat and sit and think about what you did."

"No, Lacey," Emma cried as she removed her coat and sat in the chair.

"I'll come back in about thirty minutes and we'll talk." It took all of Lacey's strength to walk out the door. Emma's wails followed her.

"Lacey!" Emma screamed.

She sat at the kitchen table and buried her face in her hands. How did parents do this? It was pure torture, but she had to start setting boundaries for Emma. She just never dreamed how hard it would be.

"Lacey," Emma kept calling.

The sobs and calling suddenly stopped, and Lacey glanced up, waiting for Emma to walk into the kitchen. But she didn't. Lacey didn't know what she would do if Emma disobeyed her now. Her luck held, and the house grew quiet. After fifteen minutes, Lacey could stand it no longer. She slowly made her way to Emma's room.

Her sister was still in the chair, her head bent as if she was studying her sneakers. She looked up when Lacey entered.

"Can I get up now?"

Lacey sat on the bed and patted the spot next to her. "Let's talk."

Emma climbed up beside her, her eyes still watery, and Lacey felt a catch in her throat. She hated this part.

"Do you know what you did wrong?"

Emma nodded. "But Mr. Gabe doesn't mind me coming over. We talked."

Lacey didn't want to remind her sister that she had done all the talking. "That's not the point. I asked you not to go over to Gabe's."

"But…"

"Emma, sweetie, Dad put me in charge of you and your welfare, and your well-being is my top priority. When you continue to disobey me, I feel as if I have failed in my promise."

"No, Lacey." Emma leaned into her, her face against Lacey's arm. "I love you."

Lacey wrapped her arms around her sister. "I know you do. And I love you. That's the reason I'm here."

"I didn't mean to disobey. You were on the phone and I went outside and heard Pepper and Mr. Gabe. I wanted to see what they were doing. I forgot, Lacey. I forgot what you said. I didn't do it on purpose. I'm sorry."

Lacey hugged Emma tightly. "We're going to make new rules. From now on, when you hear Pepper I want you to come to me and tell me, and then we'll decide if you can go over and visit the dog. That's the way it's going to be, Emma. Do you understand?"

Emma nodded and looked up at Lacey. "Pepper is sick and Mr. Gabe's gonna take her to the doctor. Can we go see Pepper tomorrow?"

"I'll go over and ask Gabe, but we have to respect his wishes."

"'Kay."

"Get your crayons and pencils and drawing stuff out, and I'll go over and talk to Gabe."

Emma jumped off the bed. "I'll draw a picture of Pepper. Are we going to the park later?"

"No. That's part of your punishment. I'm not rewarding you with fun time."

"Oh." Lacey expected more tears, but Emma acquiesced easily, which Lacey was more than grateful for. She was holding on by a thread with her parenting skills.

"I'll be back in a few minutes."

Emma was busy pulling things out of a drawer as Lacey walked out. Lacey had to apologize to Gabe one more time and see exactly how he felt about Emma invading his privacy. And she had to thank him for removing the board.

GABE PLANNED TO give Pepper a few more minutes and then he would take her inside. He wasn't sure when he realized someone was standing there, but he felt a strong presence and turned his head. It was the crazy lady. Now what?

She stepped onto his deck. "I'm sorry Emma came over here and disturbed you."

He frowned. "Who's Emma?"

She blinked, as if she was caught in the headlights of something disturbing. "She's...my sister. The little girl who is always coming into your yard. Against your wishes."

"Oh." He was losing his mind, and he hated that she was reminding him how out of touch he was.

She motioned toward the gate. "Thanks for removing the board."

"Yeah. I shouldn't have done that."

What did she want? Couldn't she see he was having trouble making conversation?

Pepper whimpered, and she went to the dog and squatted next to her. "Is Pepper sick?"

Go away, he screamed inside his head. But then he heard words coming out of his mouth. "She has cancer."

"Oh. I'm sorry." She patted the dog and seemed generally concerned. But his perception was way off. "Is there any help for her?"

He rubbed his hands together, not wanting to talk, but once again words erupted from his throat. "No. The vet said it's time to put her to sleep. But she was my son's dog and I can't do that."

She continued to pat the dog. "She's trembling in pain. You have to do something. You can't just leave her like this."

"She's the last thing I have of my son. If she goes, I…"

She got up and knelt in front of him. He looked into green eyes as bright and shining as anything he'd ever seen. Was that a tear he glimpsed?

"She's not the last thing you have of your son." She placed a hand over her heart. "In here you have many memories that no one and nothing can take from you, not Pepper's death or anything on this earth. That love, that feeling, will always be with you."

His gaze narrowed on her face and he saw her for the first time, really saw her. Her hair was blond, a beautiful natural color, and it was short, kind of kicked up at the back and curled around her face. It gave her a young

Meg Ryan appeal.... He had no idea where that thought came from.

"I'm sorry, I don't know your name. I'm a little out of touch."

"It's Lacey."

A pretty name for a pretty woman. He shook his head. "You don't understand."

"I do. I lost my father. The one and only safety net I had in my life, and suddenly all that security was gone. It's been hard holding it together for Emma. I know your situation is different, but you can't continue to let this dog suffer. Do the humane thing like the vet suggested."

"I've been trying to do that, but something always stops me."

"I will go with you if that will help."

He looked at her again. He was a man and strong enough to handle anything. He'd dealt with his son's death. Why was he so frightened of what would happen to him once Pepper was gone? Suddenly he saw a lifeline in her eyes. That was the way he saw it, and he took it, because it was the only thing he had at the moment.

"Thank you. I...I would appreciate that."

She went back to Pepper. "Do you have anything to give her for pain?"

"The vet gave me some injections. I only have one left."

Lacey sat next to the dog and stroked her. "She really needs something."

He stood and walked into the house, knowing once he gave Pepper the injection, he would have to take her to the vet. It was time.

The woman was still there when he came back. She watched as he gave Pepper the injection. The dog drifted into sleep.

"When do you want to take her in?"

"The medication lasts a little over twenty-four hours. Probably tomorrow or when the vet has an opening." He made the decision and he wasn't panicking, because this woman, this crazy woman as he'd called her, had reached out a hand when he'd desperately needed it.

"Do you mind if Emma says goodbye to Pepper? She's very fond of her, and I don't know how she's going to take this."

He ran a hand through his hair. "Do whatever you feel is best."

"Thanks. You're doing the right thing. I'll...I'll talk to you tomorrow."

Was he doing the right thing? Then why did he feel as if he was in a deep dark hole without any chance for survival?

As she left, he wondered what had just happened. He'd talked so much in the past few minutes that his throat burned. And he realized how much he missed talking. How he missed a lot of things. Maybe there was a light at the end of his long dark tunnel. A green light.

LACEY STOOD ON her patio and took a deep breath. She needed it to calm her emotions before she went into the house. Gabe's pain touched her heart. She feared this might be the last straw for him. But she would do everything she could to help him. She was just glad he was in a receptive mood, because he didn't need to go through this alone.

She knew about loneliness, death, suffering and the unimaginable pain that went along with them. Maybe they could find solace together. She was still reeling from him talking to her. He had a deep, strong voice, and she could picture him in a courtroom. There wasn't much on this earth he couldn't handle, she imagined, except the death of his son.

Shivering, she wrapped her arms around her waist. Soon there had to be some relief for Gabe. He couldn't continue to live the way he had been, and the fact that he'd actually confided in her gave her hope. She wiped away an errant tear.

Now she had another problem. How was she going to tell Emma about Pepper? Once again, death was going to derail them for a short time. It was too much, though. Too much for a six-year-old girl to handle. Too much for a twenty-eight-year-old woman to handle. And definitely too much for the man next door to handle.

She opened the door and went inside. Emma sat at the table, drawing.

Emma lifted her head. "Look. I drew a picture of Pepper."

Lacey removed her jacket and stared at the black dog on the paper with the blue sky, green grass and tall trees. A happy scene.

How was she going to tell Emma?

"Very nice."

"Did you talk to Mr. Gabe?"

"Yes, and—"

The doorbell rang, interrupting her. She hurried to answer it, glad for the reprieve. Bradley Wilson and his son Brad stood on the doorstep.

"Hi, Lacey," Bradley said. "My son has something to say to Emma."

Emma ran into the room. Lacey caught her before she could do anything stupid. "Brad has come to see you."

"I don't want to see him," Emma replied. "I want to hit him."

Bradley poked his son.

"Emma, I'm sorry I ruined your Christmas," Brad said, as if he'd memorized the words or as if someone had quoted them to him.

Emma glared at him and Lacey bent and whispered in her ear, "Say thank-you for the apology."

Now Emma glared at her. Lacey lifted an eyebrow and Emma repeated the words. At the end she tacked on, "I still want to hit you."

"Don't worry, Emma," Bradley said. "Brad has asked Santa for an Xbox, and since he believes there is no Santa and has told this to other children, he won't be getting an Xbox."

"Dad!" Brad wailed.

Bradley looked at Lacey. "I'm really sorry about this."

"Thank you, and thanks for the apology."

They walked off, and Lacey and Emma went into the living room. "That was nice of Brad."

"He's a big baby."

"Emma…"

"It's true, Lacey. He's crying like a baby 'cause he's not gonna get an Xbox."

Lacey sat on the sofa, flipping through the imaginary book in her head. "Let's talk about belief."

Emma hopped up beside her. "Why?"

"Because belief can be a powerful thing. If you believe strong enough, long enough, wonderful things can happen."

"Like maybe there really is a Santa."

Lacey tucked a stray curl behind Emma's ear. "Could be. All you have to do is believe."

"You're getting really weird, Lacey."

Lacey kissed the tip of Emma's nose. "Just believe, that's all you have to do."

"I'll try. But I know the truth and I can't forget it."

Lacey pulled Emma onto her lap, knowing they had to talk about something much more important. She had to tell Emma about Pepper.

Chapter Five

"Sweetie—"

"Are you mad at me, Lacey?" Emma interrupted, resting the side of her face against Lacey's chest.

"No, I'm not mad at you."

"But you punished me."

That obviously stung a little. "Why did I do that?"

Emma played with the watch on Lacey's wrist. "'Cause…'cause I disobeyed."

"Yes, you did. But we talked about it and you're not going to do that again, right?"

"Mmm-hmm."

It was just too difficult to punish Emma, especially at this grieving time in their lives. Maybe she would get better as the years rolled on. Even though Lacey knew she had to be the adult and set rules and boundaries, she would rather that she and Emma be friends instead of Lacey being the stern disciplinarian.

"Lacey, Pepper is really sick," Emma said, and it brought Lacey back to the present problem.

"Yes, she is."

"But Mr. Gabe is going to take her to the doctor and the doctor will make her all better."

Lacey tightened her arms around Emma. "I talked to Gabe, and Pepper is not going to get better."

Emma looked up at her. "Why not?"

Lacey swallowed and glanced toward the ceiling. *I could use a little help here.*

"Why, Lacey?"

"Because like you said, Pepper is really sick. She... she has cancer."

Emma's eyes rounded. "Like Daddy had?"

Their father had died of prostate cancer, which he had let go on too long. Taking care of Mona and Emma, he'd neglected his own health. The doctors had operated, but it had been too late. The cancer had spread.

"There are all kinds of cancer. I'm not sure what kind Pepper has, but it's bad."

"Is she going to die?"

The book in Lacey's head was closed, and there wasn't any reason to flip through it, because there was no answer. She'd read so many books about death and grief, and she still didn't have the answer or the words to make the pain better. The person just had to deal with it. That was the really hard part, especially for a child.

She looked into Emma's troubled green eyes. "Yes, Pepper is going to die."

"No." Emma buried her face in Lacey's chest and cried. All Lacey could do was hold her and pray for the right words. Loud sobs racked Emma's little body, and Lacey's eyes filled with tears as she waited for the cries to subside.

She rubbed Emma's back. "Pepper is in a lot of pain."

Emma raised her head, wiping away tears. "I know. She shakes."

Lacey drew in a deep breath. "Gabe is going to take her to a doctor, but he won't be bringing her back."

Emma's eyes rounded even more. "Is the doctor going to put her to sleep?"

Lacey was startled at the question. She'd had no idea Emma knew about such things. "How did you know that?"

"Last year, Jimmy's cousin's dog had to be put to sleep. He was real sick, too. Jimmy said the doctor took away his pain and now he's in heaven."

Thank you. She glanced briefly toward the ceiling.

"That's what the vet is going to do for Pepper."

"Then he'll go to heaven and be with Zack?"

Lacey squeezed her sister, amazed at her insight. "Yes, sweetie. Pepper will go and be with Zack now."

"I have to say goodbye." Emma began to scramble from her lap, but Lacey caught her.

"Not today. Gabe is taking this really bad, so we have to let him have his privacy. Please understand that, Emma."

Emma twisted her hands. "But…"

"You have school tomorrow, and when you get home you can spend time with Pepper and say goodbye. Gabe said you could."

"'Kay." Emma leaned against her and Lacey just held her as they both came to grips with the situation.

They ate dinner in silence, and then Lacey got Emma's clothes and backpack ready for school the following day. Then they settled in to watch some TV, but Lacey's thoughts were with the man next door. He really didn't need to be alone. If she went over there, she felt sure her visit would be met with a big scowl. She would take baby steps with Gabe. In the days ahead she would make sure he wasn't alone.

THE NEXT MORNING on the way to school Emma said, "Don't be late today."

"I'm never late," Lacey replied as she pulled into the

parking lot of the Horseshoe school. Since the town was small, grades one through twelve were housed in one big building shaped like a horseshoe. There were portable buildings to the side for pre-K and kindergarten. A gym and cafeteria were situated at the end of the horseshoe. The metal buildings with the half-brick front had been there for years. Green shrubs enhanced the front. In the spring, colorful flowers would be blooming in the flowerbeds, planted by the agriculture teacher, Mr. Schuldt.

Kids ran to the front door so they could make it to their classrooms before the bell rang. Emma climbed out and so did Lacey.

"Be good today and be nice to your playmates." She kissed her sister.

Emma fidgeted.

"Everything will be fine. I'll be here early if that will make you feel better."

"'Kay. Love you." Emma followed the children into the school, her black-and-purple backpack flopping on her back.

Lacey got in the car and drove home, hoping Emma wouldn't dwell on Pepper too much today. She seemed to be okay with what was happening, and Lacey wanted it to stay that way.

As she pulled into her driveway, she noticed everything was quiet at Gabe's. No banging or sounds anywhere, which was unusual. He was usually outside by now working on something.

She made her way into her house, put her purse on the table and walked over to his deck. He wasn't there. She knocked and got no answer. Everything was quiet inside. Where was he?

She went back to her house and across the yard to his front door. Again, she got no answer. She knew she was trespassing, but she didn't care. Her only thought was of Gabe and his mental state. Without thinking it to death, she opened the double gates by the garage. That was when she heard the sound. A saw or a drill. She didn't know which, but Gabe was working in his garage.

When she tried the garage's side door, it opened easily and the sound was much louder. She stepped inside and saw Gabe working on a large box. Was that a coffin? Yes, there was no mistaking it. He'd made a coffin for Pepper. Her chest ached at the sadness of it all.

He turned off the sander and set it on the floor. As he did, he noticed her. She expected him to be startled or surprised, but he was neither. He just went back to working on the box.

Walking closer, she said, "I knocked, but you didn't answer."

He rubbed the plywood with a rag. "Did you want something?"

She curled her hands into fists. He was acting as if they hadn't talked yesterday, as if they hadn't shared something special, as if he wanted her out of his garage. That wasn't happening. He was putting up every defense he could to keep her away so he could keep feeling the pain. That wasn't happening, either.

"You've made a coffin for Pepper."

"Yes. I'm not just going to throw her in the ground."

The whole attitude thing had resurfaced, but she was good at kicking attitude.

"Did you call the vet?"

"Uh…"

She held up a hand. "Please, let's not go back to the old animosity. Did you call the vet?"

He stopped rubbing the wood. "I was feeling down last night, but today I have everything under control."

"Yeah, I can see that." She glanced at his appearance. He had on the same clothes as yesterday and he hadn't shaved. "Have you been to bed at all?"

He went back to fiddling with the wood. "I don't sleep much."

"Because that's when you dream."

He stared at her. "You don't know anything about me."

"I don't have to. I know you're barely hanging on emotionally, and you don't sleep because that's when you dream about your son. I've been there and I'm still there, and I'm still trying to cope. And I have to because I have a little girl who needs me."

"Well, I don't have anyone, so would you please leave me alone?"

She stepped closer to him. "No, sorry. I can't do that. I promised you I would be here to help you with Pepper."

Their eyes locked. His eyes were cold and dark, emitting a message that she received all too well, but it still didn't deter her.

"I relieve you of that promise."

She shook her head. "I'm not going anywhere."

"This is my house, and I'm asking you to leave." Anger flashed in his eyes. Her first instinct was to turn and walk away and let him live in all the pain he had created. But something beyond her control made her lay her hand on the box.

"This is really nice. Zack would be very proud of his father."

Gabe froze, just as she had expected. She'd said Zack's name on purpose, because it was the only thing that caught his attention.

"Are you dense? Get out of my garage."

A tremor ran through her, and she knew she couldn't continue to be stronger than she was. It was taking everything she had to stand her ground. She didn't know what would have happened next if Pepper hadn't come into the garage.

"Oh, Pepper is better." She went to the dog and stroked her.

Gabe glared at Lacey and she continued to pet the dog.

"The medication helps," he said so low that she barely caught it.

"Did you call the vet?" she asked one more time.

"Yes. And he said he will come to the house in the morning at ten and do the procedure here."

"That would be much better and less stressful on Pepper. And you."

"I'm not worried about me," he snapped.

"I'm well aware of that."

Pepper whimpered.

Lacey hugged her. "Are you in pain, girl?"

"She wants to go outside." He wiped his hands on a rag. "Come on, Pep. We'll go outside." Gabe walked past Lacey through a door into a utility room. Pepper trailed behind, but she wobbled. It was clear she was very weak.

Lacey had the choice either to walk out the garage door and retreat to her house or to follow them. She did the latter. In the kitchen, Pepper's strength gave way and she sank to the floor. Gabe picked her up as if she weighed no more than a feather and carried her out the back door.

Lacey was dumbstruck by the scene before her. The kitchen had a table and one chair. The counters were bare; nothing was on them. It looked as if no one lived there, except for the dog dishes on the floor. She gasped as she saw the wall.

Photos of a brown-haired little boy covered it, from

the day he was born until the day he'd died. Zack in a crib, crawling, walking and holding on to Gabe's fingers, on a tricycle, then a bicycle, a skateboard and doing numerous other activities. Zack's life was on this wall.

She peeked through the doorway into the living room. There was a sofa, chair and a TV on a box, but she didn't think it was plugged in. And another wall dedicated to Zack. Gabe had made his house a shrine to his son. It was the most depressing thing Lacey had ever seen. She shook off the morbid feeling and went outside.

Pepper was curled up in her bed and Gabe sat in a lawn chair, watching her. Lacey took the other chair and they sat in silence, much like Gabe and Emma had yesterday.

Pepper laid her face off the side of the bed and kept a close eye on the backyard. "She likes it out here," Lacey said.

"Yes, but sometimes it's too cold." His voice was similar to yesterday, so she kept talking.

"I didn't know a vet would come to the house."

"I didn't either, but I like the idea much better than Pepper being in a strange place."

Since he seemed to be in a better mood, she suggested, "I can sit with Pepper if you'd like to take a nap or...a shower."

He rested his elbows on his knees and rubbed his hands together. She waited for sharp words to hit her.

"I...I think I will take a shower." He went into the house without another word.

Lacey exhaled deeply. How did the man keep going without sleep? And then it dawned on her that that was the reason he was so grouchy. She might be in over her head with Gabe, but she couldn't make herself turn away from someone in need.

Pepper moaned and stretched out. Lacey eased to the deck and sat by her, stroking her. The poor thing was in so much pain, She was glad Gabe had made the right decision for the dog. She just hoped it was the right one for Gabe.

GABE SHOWERED QUICKLY and decided to shave. The crazy lady was annoying the crap out of him, but in a way she was holding him accountable for his actions. He didn't need her telling him what to do. He didn't need her at all. He…was lying to himself. He'd reached out to her last night because he was losing control of his faculties. There was only one thing to do concerning Pepper, and he had needed someone to give him that push. It just happened to be the lady next door. Now he had to get rid of her, because he could handle this all by himself.

After changing into clean clothes, he went back outside. He paused in the doorway. She was sitting on the deck talking to Pepper.

"I bet you'd like to chase squirrels. My friend had a dog, and when we took her to the park she would spend all her time chasing squirrels. It made her happy." Pepper raised her head as if she understood, and the woman kept talking. "Oh, you like squirrels." Her voice dropped to a tone of sadness. "I'm sorry you're in so much pain, but it will get better soon. And there are a lot of squirrels in heaven, I'm sure."

"Do you really think she understands you?" He couldn't keep the derision out of his voice.

She looked at him. "I choose to believe she does, Mr. Garrison. It's all about belief."

He returned to his chair. "Please don't talk to me about religion."

"Oh, please, like I would dare." She pushed to her

feet, and he couldn't drag his eyes away from her slim body. That surprised him, because he didn't really want to see her. He tried to remember her name and couldn't.

"I'm talking about believing that there is a better place for us when we die. I have to believe that because I know my father is in a better place than the hell he was in here on earth." Her voice wavered, and he felt a catch in his throat, an emotion he hadn't felt in ages.

"I'm sorry about your father," he found himself saying. "I didn't know him all that well, but he was a good neighbor."

She sat in the chair. "Yes, my father was an exceptional man. I miss him every day, and I'm so afraid of doing all the wrong things with Emma."

"She seems well-adjusted and happy."

"I'm sorry she bothers you so much, but she loves Pepper. I've been thinking about getting her a dog."

He was supposed to say something here, but he wasn't sure what it was. The kid did bother him and he really did want to be alone. But he didn't voice his real feelings, because for the first time in two years he felt someone else's pain, and it blindsided him. Maybe into reality. Maybe into accepting that he had to go on. That was his only choice, and it came from a woman who knew about grief.

All of a sudden he didn't want to get rid of her. He wanted to keep talking. But what would that accomplish? He had to make her see that he didn't need her. Or anyone.

Chapter Six

Gabe got to his feet. "Pepper doesn't need a babysitter. She'll lay out here and enjoy the fresh air. I have to finish the box, but I'll check on her every now and then." He looked directly at Lacey. "And I'm sure you have things to do at your own house."

"Actually, I have laundry waiting for me." Lacey stood and faced him, even though it was like facing a towering inferno of attitude that was leveled right at her. "I'll go on one condition."

"I don't do conditions."

She ignored the warning in his voice. "I'll go if you come and eat a sandwich with me at lunch."

"I don't eat at a set time. I eat when I get hungry and I never watch the clock."

She placed her hands on her hips. "Today at twelve."

His eyes darkened. "Listen…hell. I don't even remember your name."

"It's Lacey," she replied with as much patience as she could find.

"Lacey," he said with a husky growl that seemed to come from somewhere deep within him. "I am not coming to your house for lunch at twelve or ever."

She sat back down.

"What are you doing?"

"If you're not coming, then I'll just stay here. I have the whole day free. Isn't that nice?"

By the narrowing of his eyes it was clear he considered it anything but nice. He threw up his hands. "Okay, okay. I'll come over at noon. Now will you please leave?"

Once again she stood, her eyes catching his. "Since you asked so politely, I'll go. See you at noon." She turned and walked toward the gate, forcing herself not to look back at the scowl on his face. But there was a moment of victory in her heart. She'd won this round.

She went inside and sat at the kitchen table. All those creepy-crawly doubts niggled her. What was she doing? She was trying to help someone else when some days she was barely holding it together herself. But there was no one else to help Gabe. She remembered those days after her dad had passed, the horrible sadness, the debilitating pain and trying to hold it all together for Emma. They'd come a long way in five months, but occasionally they needed a helping hand, and the people of Horseshoe had been very kind to them. And she had to be kind to Gabe. It was that simple for her.

She stripped the beds and put the sheets in the washing machine. All the while she was thinking she should fix something appetizing for lunch. Since her culinary skills were limited, she called Angie.

She came straight to the point. "I need help with a cooking problem."

"Okay. I need details."

"I have ham and cheese. How do I make that into something special in a sandwich?"

"Grill it in a frying pan like a grilled cheese. Use butter." Angie went through the process step by step, and Lacey wrote it down. "Serve with a pickle, chips and beverage of your choice, and you have an appetizing lunch."

"Thank you. This sounds simple—so simple I think I can accomplish it."

Angie laughed. "Call if you run into a problem."

Lacey hung up and went to work. By noon she had the sandwiches on a plate without a burn mark on them. She added cherry tomatoes, a pickle and chips, then waited for Gabe. At five minutes after twelve she had a sneaking suspicion he wasn't coming. With her back to the stove, she tapped her foot, counting off the minutes on the coffee mug–shaped wall clock. When the big hand hit the quarter hour, she marched to the door.

She yanked it open and jumped back. Gabe stood with his hand in the air, getting ready to knock.

His perpetual scowl was firmly in place. "I told you I don't watch a clock. I was washing my hands in the kitchen when I noticed the time, so I came without changing clothes because I knew you would be storming over if I didn't."

Sawdust coated his jeans and a brown stain marred his T-shirt. She wanted to laugh. She'd made an impression. Even though he might not admit it, he didn't want to upset her. He was thinking about other people, and that was good.

She stepped aside and opened the door wider, letting his remarks fade away. "Are you still working on the box?" she asked just to make conversation.

Before coming in, he brushed the sawdust from his jeans. "I finished sanding it and stained it. It's ready."

She motioned toward a chair. "Have a seat and I'll bring our lunch. Would you rather have coffee or tea?"

"Coffee, black, but I'm really not hungry."

He was eating if she had to force it down him. She

had to suppress another laugh at the thought. Carrying the plates to the table, she noticed he'd taken a seat. At least they wouldn't have to argue about that. She hurried back with the coffee and tea and sat down.

"It's grilled ham and cheese," she said as she picked up her sandwich.

"It looks tasty, but…"

"It is, and for the record, my cooking skills are limited, so it's best to take what you're given here."

He took a sip of his coffee, his big hand engulfing the white cup. "How many fire alarms have you gone through?"

She held up one finger. "I just put them back up and they keep working."

He shook his head and the scowl on his face lessened. "I hear it regularly."

"I'm working on changing that." She nibbled on a pickle. "I had a busy life in Austin and rarely had time to develop any culinary skills." She resisted the urge to wink.

"What did you do in Austin?"

He was asking questions. That was good. She didn't know if he was doing so out of curiosity or boredom, but she'd take either. "I worked for a big party-planning company. The holidays are the busiest time of the year."

He picked up his sandwich and took a bite. "You planned parties?"

"Yes, big extravagant parties. For banks, large companies, law firms, weddings and people who wanted to make an impression. We did a lot of private parties in lavish homes."

"Isn't there food involved?"

"We hired caterers for different parties. Janine is the woman who runs the company, and I was her personal assistant. It was a fun job and I met a lot of people—nice people. I miss that part of my life."

While she'd been talking, he'd eaten the whole sandwich, probably without even realizing it. His cup was empty, so she got up to refill it.

"People just call you and tell you what they want and you do the rest?"

"That's about it."

"I worked…" His voice trailed off.

She resumed her seat. "Where did you work?"

"Doesn't matter." He clammed up, apparently realizing he was getting into personal territory.

"Dad said you were a lawyer."

Gabe studied the coffee in the cup. "A lifetime ago." He glanced toward the living room. From his chair he could see the undecorated Christmas tree. "You haven't done anything with the tree?"

"No. That's another problem. Emma doesn't want to decorate the tree."

"Why not? Kids love that kind of stuff."

Lacey pushed the chips around on her plate. "One of the Wilson kids down the street told her there isn't a Santa Claus, and now she doesn't believe and doesn't want to have Christmas."

"A kid her age should believe, and no one should take that from her."

"I agree. Kids grow up much faster these days, but I'm not giving up. I'm working on changing her mind. Did Zack like Christmas?"

Gabe stood up suddenly. "I've got to go."

She'd crossed a line, but she couldn't take the words back. She followed him.

At the door, he said, "You don't have to fuss over me. I'm fine."

"Well, you'll excuse me if I believe otherwise."

"You don't know me and I don't know you. I wish we had kept it that way."

"But we're neighbors and see each other every day. We can at least be civil."

He ran a hand through his hair. "I just want my peace. That's all."

"For today and tomorrow you'll have to put up with Emma and me. I promised her she could see Pepper this afternoon, and you're not going back on your word."

His eyes narrowed on her face, and her bravado faltered for a second. "You're very pushy, do you know that?"

"No. I'm usually a very agreeable person and easy to get along with."

He rubbed his hands together and looked at them, as if he was gauging his next words. But then he turned toward the door. "I have to go."

"Gabe, it really would help to talk about your son. I know you don't believe that, but it would. Earlier, when you spoke about my dad, it gave me a warm feeling, and if you talked about Zack it would help you."

His eyes caught hers. Once again she saw all that anguish etched across the strong lines of his face. Her breath stalled.

"I can't. Please understand that."

She wanted to reach out and touch him, hug him, comfort him in some way, but she knew that was the last thing he wanted from her.

"Gabe…"

He walked out the door.

Lacey let out a long breath and then closed the door. Gabe had taken a step forward, but now he'd taken several backward, and he still had tomorrow to get through. He wouldn't be alone, though.

PEPPER WAS ASLEEP and seemed peaceful, so Gabe went to the garage to see if the varnish on the box had dried. It hadn't. He sat on a stool and tried to collect his thoughts, tried to find reason and sanity in all the misery that clouded his mind.

It really would help to talk about your son.

How could she say that? She didn't know. He jammed both hands through his hair. Talking about Zack would tear out his heart. But then, his heart had already been destroyed. Maybe she was right. Maybe. But he still held on to every memory of his son and he held them close to his heart where no one else could ever touch them. Tomorrow, though, he would let go because it was the right thing to do. And, God help him, he couldn't do it alone.

He wasn't quite sure why it was hard to admit that, but Lacey knew. She saw right through him and she still kept pushing him even when he resisted her efforts. She was a very strong lady, and he really should be grateful she was willing to help him.

He got up. What did he care? After tomorrow, he would sink into that oblivion of complete pain, and there was no way to stop it. Not unless he reached out a hand for someone to save him. In that moment he saw her green eyes, and he shoved the image away. He didn't want to be saved. But a part of him was fighting back. A part of him was remembering what life was about. A part of him was waiting for the light to completely engulf him. If that were possible... For the first time he realized he was still living, and it was up to him to keep fighting for that light. That right.

LACEY PICKED UP Emma and they headed home. "Do you want to stop for hot chocolate and a kolach?" Emma loved the pastry brimming with different fruit mixtures in the center.

"No, Lacey. We have to go home."

Lacey knew better than to ask. Emma had her mind set on one thing—Pepper. As soon as Lacey parked in the driveway, Emma jumped out of the car and ran for the front door.

Before she opened it, Lacey said, "Remember, we talked. We're going over to Gabe's and you can stay for a little while, but then you have to come home because Gabe wants his privacy. Understand?"

Emma bobbed her head. She shot through the house like a bullet, throwing her backpack at the sofa. Lacey followed slowly.

When she reached Gabe's deck, Emma was sitting by Pepper, lovingly cuddling her. Gabe sat in his chair, watching. He'd changed clothes—that was the first thing Lacey noticed. The box must have been finished. She could only imagine how much pain it had caused him to make it. But then again, it might have been cathartic. She never knew with Gabe.

"Pepper's real sick, Mr. Gabe," Emma said.

"Yes, she is," he replied, surprising Lacey. She had expected him to remain silent.

Emma kissed the dog and then walked to Gabe. "The doctor's gonna make Pepper's pain go away?"

Gabe visibly swallowed. "Yes."

Emma crawled into the other chair and no one spoke, just like the other day. Lacey went back to her house and let Emma have this time with Pepper and Gabe. Emma was attuned to Gabe's pain, as was Lacey. She just wished he would let them in.

Later, Emma came back.

"Did you have a good visit?"

"Yes, but it's getting colder, and Mr. Gabe said I should probably go home."

"And you have homework to do."

"Yeah." Emma sat at the kitchen table.

Lacey was making dinner, but she caught her sister's somber tone and wondered if Gabe had said something to her. Lacey wiped her hands on a dish towel and walked to the table.

"Did you and Gabe talk?"

Emma shook her head. "I just helped him be sad."

"What?" Lacey was thrown by the answer.

"Gabe is sad and doesn't want to talk, so I don't talk, either. I just help him be sad."

Lacey reached over and hugged Emma. "You're getting so grown up. I'm proud of you."

Emma wiggled away as if the compliment had embarrassed her. "What's for supper? Are we going to the diner?"

"I'm making hot dogs. It's all we have. I have to go to the grocery store soon."

"It's okay. I'm not too hungry."

A sense of sadness lingered in the room. They ate supper in silence. Then Lacey had an idea. "I'm going to make Gabe a hot dog and take it to him. Get your books and start on your homework."

She left Emma at the table working on math. It was dusk, and a yellow glow had settled over the neighborhood. The air was brisk. By morning the temperature probably would be freezing. Traffic sounds softly echoed, and a dog barked in the distance.

Gabe sat on the deck as usual, and Pepper was in

her bed. Going up the steps, Lacey said, "I brought you supper."

"I'm not hungry," he said. "And it's not your job to feed me."

She let his sharp words flow over her and took a seat in the other chair with the food in her lap. "We had hot dogs, so I brought you two with a thermos of coffee. And Oreos. Everybody loves Oreos."

"I'm not everybody."

"Okay, we've established that." She handed him a hot dog wrapped in aluminum foil. He stared at it for a full thirty seconds before he took it. Unwrapping it, he took a big bite and then another.

She held out the thermos. "You might need something to wash it down."

He took it without a sharp quip. While he ate, she nibbled on an Oreo, and then offered them to him. He took the bag without a word and they ate cookies in silence.

Pepper didn't move. She was stretched out with her head on the corner of the bed. The poor thing had suffered enough, and Lacey's heart broke at what would happen tomorrow. But it was time.

"I'll be here after I drop Emma off at school in the morning."

He didn't respond.

Darkness now bathed the neighborhood, and the air had grown colder. The outdoor noises had gone quiet like the hush before a storm. Lacey didn't know whether to go or stay. Gabe was clearly struggling.

He gave her the thermos. "I…I've made up my mind, so I'll be fine. But thanks for being here and thanks for lunch today and supper. I forgot to thank you earlier."

Her throat closed up. He was so sincere, and she knew the battle inside him was ongoing. The thermos wasn't empty, so she handed it back to him. "You'll need something to finish off the cookies."

He looked up at her, and from the deck light she could feel the heat of his eyes. She wanted to reach out and hug him like she had at lunch, but she knew he wouldn't welcome that intimacy.

"Thanks," he said simply.

"You're welcome." Darkness fell like a wall, shutting out the outside world. It was just the two of them. And Pepper. Lacey wrapped her arms around her waist to ward off the chill of the night. "Even though it hurts, you're doing the right thing."

"Yeah." He twisted the thermos in his hands.

Unable to stop herself, she touched his arm. "Try to get some rest. Good night."

The muscles under her fingers tightened, and she felt his strength like a band of steel. And that epitomized Gabe. Strong. Hardened. But vulnerable. Tomorrow his nerves of steel would be tested. She left with an ache in her heart.

Chapter Seven

The next morning started with an argument. Lacey wanted Emma to wear her candy-cane tights with ankle boots, and Emma wanted to wear jeans and sneakers. In the end, Lacey gave up because she had other things on her mind.

After breakfast, Emma insisted on going to see Pepper. Lacey didn't object because she wanted to check on Gabe, too. It was cold outside—not quite freezing, with the temperature in the high 30s. She bundled up Emma and they walked next door. Gabe wasn't outside, so she knocked. He opened it almost immediately. She expected him to be unshaven and wearing the same clothes, but his long hair was slicked back and still slightly damp from a shower. And he wore clean jeans and a T-shirt. An almost forgotten longing pierced her lower abdomen.

"Uh…can Emma see Pepper one more time, please?"

He opened the door wider and Emma ran to where Pepper lay in her bed near the cabinet.

"How's Pepper?" Lacey asked Gabe, and she noticed the bags under his incredibly sad eyes. She wondered when he'd last slept.

"The shot has worn off and she's whimpering a lot."

Emma sat on the floor next to Pepper. The dog didn't even raise her head.

Emma kissed Pepper. "It'll be okay. You'll feel better soon."

"We have to go, Emma, or you'll be late for school." Lacey hated to leave Gabe, but she would be back in just a few minutes.

Emma got up and walked to her, still huddled in her coat. Blond hair peeked out from the hood. All Lacey could see were her big green eyes.

"I don't want to go. I want to stay with Pepper."

Lacey hadn't been expecting this. She had to be firm. "You have to go to school."

"Why can't I stay? Pepper wants me to."

Another unsolvable problem. Lacey did not want Emma to witness Pepper's passing. At her age, she'd dealt with enough. Lacey guided her to the one chair in the room and Emma sat.

"Sweetie, this is not something for a little girl to witness. The vet will take care of everything and Pepper will be at peace. Just know that."

Emma frowned. "I have to be here."

"Emma…" Lacey didn't know what else to say. She understood Emma loved the dog, but watching the procedure was out of the question.

"Why do you have to be here?" Gabe asked Emma, startling Lacey. She had expected him to ignore them.

"Because Lacey wouldn't let me be there when Daddy went to heaven, and I want to be here when Pepper goes to heaven."

Lacey was stunned. She'd had no idea Emma felt this way. She knelt in front of her. "Sweetie, I was in the hall with you when Daddy passed. The doctor asked us to leave the room. If I had had any idea it was his time, we would never have left. I just…just didn't know." A sob clogged her throat and she had to stop. She had failed Emma. And she'd failed herself.

"We should have been there, Lacey," Emma said.

Yes blocked her brain with so many regrettable memories. She'd done the best she could at the time, and there was no going back to change that. When the doctor had come out of the room and told them their father had passed away, she'd felt as if someone had pulled the floor out from under her and she was tumbling, tumbling down into the deepest hole of despair. But she'd had to get up. She'd had to get up for Emma.

Lacey gathered Emma into her arms and sat with her in the chair. She had to make a decision and she had no idea if it was right or wrong. But then, every decision she'd made since their father's death had been that way. She'd been going on faith, and she had to lean on it now.

Emma rested her head on Lacey's shoulder. "Please let me stay. I'll be good. I won't cry. I promise."

Lacey looked at Gabe. The lines around his eyes weren't as intense because his attention was on something other than Pepper. It was on Emma. "I'll call the vet and see what he says."

"Thank you." His offer was like a morsel of food to a starving person. She desperately needed someone to advise her, and the fact that it came from Gabe gave her a warm feeling.

Gabe went into the other room to make the call. Lacey untied Emma's hood and pushed it from her head. "If the vet says no, you have to accept that. Understand?"

Emma remained silent, and Lacey knew what that meant. *Trouble.*

"Emma…"

Emma sat up. "You don't understand."

"What don't I understand?"

Emma studied the tips of her sneakers. "I…I have to be with Pepper when she goes to heaven because I want her to take a message to Daddy."

Lacey swallowed hard and she couldn't say another word. Tears stung the backs of her eyes and threatened to erupt. The only thing Lacey knew to do was to go with the moment and let Emma have this time she thought she needed. Lacey couldn't take that away from her, even if she knew life didn't work that way. Dogs didn't take messages to heaven. But what did she know? Maybe they did. After all, it was the holiday season and a time for miracles.

Gabe came back into the room. "Dr. Morris said children are often present. It's a simple procedure and as long as the child understands what's going to happen, it usually works out well."

"Do you mind if she stays?" Lacey had to ask because Pepper was Gabe's dog and he might want to do this alone.

He shook his head.

She could tell by the softening of his eyes that he was okay with the situation, so that made things a lot easier.

"But we will have rules," Lacey said.

"You always make rules," Emma grumbled.

"Rules," Lacey stated firmly.

"'Kay."

"I'm going outside to get everything ready." Gabe laid his cell phone on the table and headed for the garage. "I want it done on the deck were Pepper loves to stay."

"I'll help." Emma tried to jump from Lacey's lap, but Lacey held tight.

Gabe paused in the doorway. "You can watch Pepper while I'm busy."

"'Kay."

Lacey unbuttoned Emma's coat. Emma sat on the floor, talking to Pepper. Lacey wondered what message her sister wanted Pepper to take to heaven. It was clear Emma didn't have closure about their dad's death. Lacey wasn't sure she did, either. They were both going through the motions of living. Just like Gabe. Hopefully, today would be a turning point for all of them. And not a step backward.

Since Gabe's phone was right there, she decided to use it to call the school about Emma. She didn't think he'd mind. Gabe was so out of touch that she was surprised he had a cell. She didn't mean to invade his privacy and it was none of her business, but when she opened the phone she noticed there were twenty-two missed calls from Kate Rebel. Lacey quickly made her call and clicked off.

Glancing out the back door, she saw him setting up a card table. The coffin was next to it on the deck. He worked thoroughly engrossed, as she'd always seen him do. Who was this woman who was desperately trying to reach him? Again, none of her business.

"Lacey, why is there only one chair?" Emma asked, getting bored as six-year-olds were known to do.

"I don't know."

Emma looked at the wall of photos. "Why are there so many pictures?"

"Gabe likes looking at his son" was the only answer she had.

"Oh." Emma turned her attention back to Pepper. "She's whimpering."

"Just stroke her. It helps her relax."

The doorbell rang. Lacey opened the back door and said to Gabe, "I think the vet's here."

Gabe came into the house. He wore just a black hoodie, but he didn't seem to be cold. "I'll let him in."

A young man in his thirties with blond hair and blue eyes followed Gabe into the kitchen. "This is Dr. Morris, and Dr. Morris, this is Lacey and Emma Carroll, my neighbors."

They shook hands and Dr. Morris looked at Emma. "So you want to be here today for Pepper?"

Emma stood up and brushed blond hair from her face. "Pepper is my friend and I want to be here when she goes to heaven."

"That's very brave," the vet told her, leaning down to Emma's level. "Do you know what an IV is?"

"Yes. My daddy had one when he was in the hospital."

"Good. I'm going to put an IV in Pepper's foreleg so I can give her medication that will gently put her to sleep."

Emma rubbed her head. "Will it hurt?"

"No."

"Then she'll go to heaven?"

"Yes. It doesn't take long. I'm going to go outside with Gabe and get everything ready, and when it's time your mother can bring you out."

"Lacey's not my mother. She's my sister," Emma quickly corrected him.

"Oh, sorry." The vet seemed confused. "You look so much alike."

"'Cause we're sisters," Emma stated.

Dr. Morris nodded. "Yes. I know now."

Without another word the two men went out onto the deck. Lacey could see them talking, and then Gabe came back into the house. He knelt down by Emma and Pepper.

"I'm going to take her outside."

Emma kissed the dog. "Goodbye, Pepper."

Lacey couldn't believe Emma was taking this so well. Tears burned her eyes, and she feared this might not have the outcome Emma wanted. But she would be here to help her. And Gabe.

Gabe picked up the dog bed with Pepper in it as if it weighed no more than his phone. She held the door open, and he carried Pepper outside to the table. Their eyes met briefly. All she could see was resignation mixed with pain.

Emma ran to her and wrapped her arms around Lacey's waist. "The doctor won't forget, will he, Lacey?"

"No, sweetie. Put your coat back on so you'll be ready."

Emma did as Lacey asked, and they waited. Gabe stood by the table, his hand on Pepper while the vet worked. Tall, strong, yet vulnerable like the big oak that was not twelve feet from him. She wanted to go to him, but she had Emma to think about. She was torn about who needed her most.

It was a relief when Gabe motioned for them to come outside. Emma shot out the door and stood next to Gabe, touching Pepper gently. Lacey stood on Gabe's other side.

The vet had his hand over the IV in Pepper's foreleg. "Say goodbye," he said, and then she noticed that with his other hand he injected the medication into the IV.

"Bye, Pepper. I love you," Emma whispered. "When you see my daddy, tell him I love him."

The words were low, but Lacey heard them. Her chest tightened in pain. Emma hadn't had the chance to say that to their father before he'd passed, and obviously it had bothered her. Lacey didn't have time to dwell on it, as she felt the man beside her tremble. She rubbed his back in reassurance, just as she would have done to Emma. He leaned into her hand as if he needed her support.

The vet removed the IV very quickly so Emma

couldn't see. Pepper took a short breath, and then she was still. Gabe stroked her head, "Goodbye, girl. You're at peace now. I'm sorry it took me so long to do…this." His voice wavered on the last word, and Lacey clutched him around the waist for reassurance.

The sun popped out like a cork from a bottle, spreading its goodness everywhere and lighting up the cold, dreary day.

"Is Pepper gone?" Emma asked.

The vet nodded. "Yes."

Emma glanced toward the bright sunshine. "She turned on the light for us."

It was a moment of relief for all of them. The vet put everything back into his bag and helped Gabe lift Pepper into the coffin, bed and all. Gabe covered her with a big quilt and positioned the lid on top.

"Would you like me to help?" the vet asked.

"No, thanks. I have it from here." The two men shook hands and Dr. Morris left.

Until that moment, Lacey hadn't noticed the big hole Gabe had dug against the wood fence. He must've stayed up all night digging.

Gabe picked up a nail gun from the deck and nailed the coffin shut. Emma watched all of this without saying a word. She seemed fine, but Lacey was skeptical.

When Gabe finished, Lacey stood at one end of the box. "I'll help you carry it."

Gabe didn't respond. He just picked up his end and they carried it to the hole. Emma followed without saying a word. Gabe jumped into the hole, and then picked up the coffin and slid it in. He had to step on the box to get out. Then he marched toward the house.

"Where you going?" Emma called.

"To get a shovel to close the hole."

Emma made a dash for their house. Lacey had no idea where she was going until she came back with a small shovel their dad had bought for her to help in the yard. Lacey wasn't going to be left out, so she went to the garage and found their father's spade.

The three of them shoveled dirt over the coffin. Lacey's arms grew tired, but Gabe and Emma kept dirt flying. Gabe stopped long enough to remove his hoodie. She could see the muscles in his arms bulging as he worked in just a black T-shirt. Lacey stopped for a moment just to watch, and then she caught herself. This was definitely not the time.

Gabe used a rake to smooth out the dirt. Pepper had been put to rest. Emma glanced toward the bright sunshine.

"Pepper's happy now."

"Yes," Lacey agreed, and thought it chased away the sadness of today. "Time to go to school."

"'Kay." Unexpectedly, Emma hugged Gabe around the waist and he tensed. "Bye, Mr. Gabe." She ran for the house.

"I'll be back as soon as I can," Lacey said to Gabe.

"There's no need. I'm fine."

She eyed that strange look on his face. He was shutting her out again. Shutting out the world because he felt safer that way.

"You did the right thing. It was a big step forward. Keep taking those steps."

"I don't need your armchair psychology. I think it's best if we went back to being—"

"What?" She lifted an eyebrow. "Neighbors? Enemies? Friends? Or maybe nothing at all would suit you best." She shook her head. "But that's not going to happen. I'll be back whether you like it or not."

She left him standing in the backyard with a befuddled look on his face. She'd never met anyone so conflicted. She supposed he had reason, but two years was long enough. Gabe had to start living again. Why that was so important to her, she had no idea. Maybe the pain in her reacted to the pain in him. Whatever it was, she was determined they would at least be friends.

THE HOUSE WAS very quiet without Pepper. Even the deck was lonely, and that loneliness went all the way to Gabe's soul. He cleaned out the garage from building the coffin and put everything away. Keeping busy kept him from thinking. After everything was back in its place, he went for a jog. He did that often to keep the memories at bay. Up and down Horseshoe streets he jogged, around the business district and to the school. He didn't stop until he was so tired he was forced to.

Breathing deeply, he sat on a curb. He purposely stayed away from his house because he didn't want Lacey to baby him, to think he needed her. He was doing fine on his own.

The people in Horseshoe avoided him and didn't speak when they saw him. They knew he wouldn't accept their hand in friendship. And that was the way he wanted it. But as he sat on the curb and listened to the thud of his heart against his ribs, his loneliness was more than painful, it was debilitating. This wasn't the normal way to live, and avoiding Lacey wasn't going to help. He stood up, feeling weary and lost. Slowly, he made his way back to his house. Back to the memories. Back to the pain.

AT FIRST, LACEY was surprised when she found Gabe gone, but then she got angry. He didn't need her, and he was making that more than clear. When she thought about it, he'd never asked for her help. She was the one who offered, so she had to take a step back and leave him alone like he wanted.

She went to the grocery store, stocked up and then came home and put everything away. Not once did she think of going to Gabe's. She couldn't believe she had been so pushy. Now she had to concentrate on Emma and her well-being.

Emma's teacher was standing outside with a group of kids when Lacey arrived at the school. That wasn't a good sign. Mrs. Fillmore obviously had more complaints about Emma's behavior, which seemed to happen about once a week.

Getting out of her car, Lacey took a deep breath and said hello to the teacher. The woman wasn't frowning like she usually was.

"Good afternoon, Lacey," Mrs. Fillmore said cheerily.

Lacey wondered what had happened to make the teacher so happy.

"Good afternoon."

Mrs. Fillmore was somewhere in her forties with brown highlighted hair and a shaken–soda can personality, bubbly and lively. The kids loved her. "I wasn't sure what to expect when Emma returned to class today. The death of a beloved pet is traumatic for a child."

"What happened?" Lacey asked.

"She came into the classroom and took her seat. I was just going to resume the class when she raised her hand. She wanted to know if she could tell the class about Pepper. I was hesitant at first, but agreed. I can't tell you how well it went. It was marvelous. She opened up to the kids and they responded. It was wonderful to see. I hope the old Emma is back. I'm almost positive she is."

Lacey could hardly believe her ears. "Emma stood up in front of the class and spoke?"

Mrs. Fillmore nodded. "She did. I'm so happy to give you good news for a change."

"And I'm happy to hear it."

Childish giggles echoed, and Lacey glanced to where Emma was standing with Jimmy and two other kids. She was actually talking with them and not frowning or hitting. When Emma saw Lacey, she came running over with the little girl Lacey recognized from the Christmas-tree lot.

"Just wanted to give you the good news," Mrs. Fillmore said, and walked back into the school.

"Thanks," Lacey called after her.

"Lacey, this is Bailey. Look what she gave me." Emma twisted her wrist and Lacey saw a stretchy band with sparkles that a lot of little girls were wearing. "Isn't it pretty?"

"Yes. That was very nice of Bailey."

"Can she come play with me sometime?"

Yes, yes, yes! Lacey wanted to shout. It was the best news she'd heard in a while. Emma was making friends again, fitting in.

"If her mother says it's okay."

"Bye, Bailey." Emma waved as the little girl ran off. "Don't forget to ask your mommy."

Lacey had hoped for a miracle and she'd gotten one. For Emma. But Gabe's miracle was yet to come.

Chapter Eight

Gabe sat looking at his backyard. The large oak to the right had died during the drought of 2011. Tomorrow he would cut it down. It would be his goal for the week. His eyes slid over to the fresh mound of dirt on the left.

Rest in peace, girl.

He'd prolonged her life more than he should have, because he'd known that once he let go of Pepper he would have to face reality. A reality that was too dark and disturbing to even think about, so he had kept putting it off to another day.

If Lacey hadn't pushed him, Pepper would still be in pain. He needed to thank her for that, but she probably wasn't going to speak to him anytime soon. Maybe that wasn't a bad thing. He couldn't make himself believe that, though. He ran both hands through his hair with a long sigh.

Voices caught his attention, and he glanced up to see Emma and Lacey coming through the gate. Emma bounded up the steps with a handful of yellow flowers. They looked like daisies. She walked right up to him.

"Do you mind if we put flowers on Pepper's grave?"

He swallowed. "No."

Lacey stood in the yard, and he noticed that hurt look

in her eyes. Damn! He hadn't meant to hurt her, but then what had he expected?

Jumping down the steps, Emma went to Lacey and they walked to the grave. Emma knelt down and carefully placed the flowers. She said something to Lacey, but Gabe couldn't catch it. It was getting colder again, and Lacey pulled her brown jacket tighter around her. Taking the child's hand, she led her back to the gate.

He had a new ache in his gut, an unfamiliar one he didn't like. She had been nothing but kind to him and he had hurt her in return. Drawing in a deep breath, he called, "Lacey."

She stopped with a puzzled look in her green eyes.

"Could we talk for a minute?"

"I suppose." She looked down at Emma. "Go start your homework and I'll be there in a minute."

The child darted off and he made his way to Lacey. "I'm sorry I bailed on you today."

She brushed blond hair from her forehead. "Why did you?"

He studied the wood grain on the weather-worn fence. "I was feeling claustrophobic and had to get away and be by myself. I know you don't understand that, but it was something I had to do. I walked around Horseshoe until I couldn't breathe, then I sat on a curb and tried to remember exactly what I was doing. Nothing makes much sense to me. I think you already know that."

"Yes." She shoved her hands into the pockets of her jacket. "I was just worried about you, that's all. And I shouldn't be because I barely know you. But you're hurting and I can identify with that. If I'm overstepping my bounds, I'm sorry."

Staring into her eyes, he wondered how she could know him so well. No one understood him. Not his ex-wife. Or his sister. Or his friends. But she seemed to reach a part of him that he kept hidden. Maybe that was why he'd had to get away. He hadn't wanted to expose that part of himself.

"I...I..."

She touched his arm and he stiffened. She'd done that once before and it had thrown him off guard. Human contact was alien to him now, but it seemed natural when she did it.

"It's okay. I understand. Take all the time you need. I'm right next door if you need anything." She turned and walked to her house.

He sucked in the cool air, and it chilled all the aches and pains inside him. Would there ever be an end to his agony? Maybe not, but he would not hurt Lacey again.

WHEN SUPPER WAS finished, Lacey sent Emma to take a bath, and afterward Lacey brushed Emma's long hair.

"You had fun in school today?"

Lacey sat on Emma's bed, and Emma stood between her legs. "Yes. I like Bailey."

"I'm glad you found a friend."

"She gave me something. I need to give her something back. You make my bows. Can you make her a bow?"

"I certainly will, but not tonight."

"Ouch. You're pulling my hair."

"Sorry, snuggle bunny." Lacey patted the bed beside her. "Let's talk for a minute."

Emma groaned as she climbed onto the bed. "What did I do?"

Lacey put her arm around her sister. "You didn't do anything wrong. I just want to tell you how proud I am of the way you handled today."

Emma rested against her. "Oh."

"Sweetie, you do understand why we weren't in the room when Daddy passed?"

"Yeah. But it's okay now."

"'Cause Daddy knows you love him?"

Emma drew back, her eyes big. "How do you know that?"

Lacey squeezed her. "Haven't you figured out by now that I know everything?"

"You're weird, Lacey."

"If you have questions, I'll try to answer them."

Emma burrowed farther into her. "Daddy's never coming back, is he?"

Lacey's voice was clogged with tears, and she didn't bother to look for an answer in her imaginary book. She had to go with the feeling in her heart. "No...no, sweetie. He's never coming back." She laid her hand on Emma's chest. "But he's right there." Then she laid her hand on her chest. "And he's right here. He's with us all the time in spirit."

"Is Pepper there, too?"

"You bet." She kissed her sister's forehead. "It's homework time."

"Aw, jeez."

"You have math problems to do."

Emma made a face. "I hate math."

"Get your books and you can work at the kitchen table."

Emma trailed behind her, grumbling as they made their way to the kitchen. Lacey set up everything and Emma went to work.

"Sweetie, I'm going next door for a minute."

"'Kay."

She couldn't get Gabe out of her mind. He'd said he was sorry and that meant a lot to her. Caught off guard, she'd failed to thank him for letting Emma stay today, and she needed to do that. Maybe it was just another reason to see him. Or maybe she was pushy.

It was already dark and she didn't like leaving Emma, but she'd only be gone a few minutes. She found her way to the deck, but the light wasn't on. Had he gone to bed? She tapped on the door, but he didn't answer. She tried the screen door and it opened, as did the door.

"Gabe," she called into the dark house. Still no response. A light was coming from the living room—a very dim light. Acting braver than she was feeling, she walked into the kitchen and then into the living room. A lamp was on next to the TV. Gabe sat on the sofa in jeans and a black T-shirt. His head was tilted back, and his bare feet were outstretched.

"Gabe," she said tentatively. He immediately raised himself up.

"Lacey. What are you doing here?"

"I called, but you didn't hear me, and I got worried."

He swiped a hand through his hair. "I must've been half-asleep."

She wanted to ask if he was okay, but she knew better. He was tired of that question. "I won't stay. I just wanted to thank you for letting Emma stay today. It has made a world of difference in her attitude. I never realized she needed to tell our father she loved him before he passed."

"Yeah. It seemed important to her. I'm glad it helped."

Going where brave angels feared to tread, she sat beside him without an invitation. "Did it help you?"

He lifted an eyebrow. "Doing your psychology thing again?"

She stood up. "I was only trying to help. I'll leave you alone." It was the last thing she wanted to do, because she could hear the panic in his voice. But she wasn't sure how to help him other than to annoy him, which was how it usually turned out. She took a step toward the kitchen.

"I don't know what to do with myself." The words came out low and husky, but Lacey heard them. "I go outside and then I come back in. I feel lost, without any direction, like a car without a steering wheel. I don't know where to go or where to turn. I've lost the most important part of myself. I've lost my son. Zack is dead." The last word came out on a choked sob, and more sobs followed.

At the gut-wrenching sound, Lacey's heart plummeted to the pit of her stomach, and she sat by him again, wanting to give him some sort of comfort. "Gabe…"

"Zack is dead."

She wrapped her arms around him, and he sobbed into her chest, saying the words over and over. Her heart rate was dangerously close to overload at the pain in his voice, and she didn't know what else to do. Clearly, he had never said the words out loud. Her guess was that he'd never openly cried over the death of his son. He had never allowed himself that weakness.

His arms gripped her, and he held on as if she were his anchor. His sobs did a number on her control and she was glad when he silently laid his head on her shoulder. Suddenly, he leaned away, wiping away the telltale tears. "Sorry. I lost it for a minute."

"Is this the first time you've cried?"

He rested his head against the sofa. "Yes. My ex-wife couldn't understand why I didn't cry. She called me hard and unfeeling. She called me a lot of things, but I knew if I allowed myself that weakness, Zack's death would be real, and I didn't want it to be real."

She stroked his arm, and he didn't pull away.

"Zack was a mischievous, happy kid, always laughing, always teasing. I don't understand how someone with so much life in him can suddenly be gone."

"We'll never have an answer for that."

"No, we won't. I kept holding on to Pepper, determined not to accept the reality. But…my son is dead and he's never coming back." He said the words with a finality that was as real as it could get. Lacey thought it strange that she'd had this same conversation with Emma just a few minutes ago.

"No." She laid her hand on his chest, as she had Emma. "But he lives in here."

"Yeah." He caught her hand and entwined his fingers with hers. Her heart skipped a beat. "Thanks for listening. Saying those words was long overdue."

He closed his eyes and she waited for him to speak again, but there was only silence. Then his chest rose and fell quietly. He had drifted into sleep—a much-needed sleep. Removing her hand, she reached for the blanket at the end of the sofa and spread it over him. She didn't want to wake him because he desperately needed to sleep. The urge to kiss him was strong, and she didn't know why. She couldn't be attracted to him. There was no future with Gabe Garrison. He lived in the past, and she had a six-year-old to raise. But there was a connection she couldn't deny.

She let herself out of the house and locked the door as she left, feeling good that Gabe had finally admitted something he'd been denying for two solid years. His son was gone and he had to go on living. Maybe there was hope for him.

GABE WOKE UP to a surreal feeling. For a moment he didn't know where he was, but then he saw the photos on the wall and all that pain blindsided him. It wasn't like before, though. Something was different.

Sitting up, he realized there was a blanket over him. And then it all came back. Lacey. The tears. Oh, God. He'd made a fool of himself. Strangely, he didn't feel like a fool. He felt revitalized. He got to his feet and an old urge hit him. He wanted coffee. For years, that had been the first thing he'd done every morning. Lately, he hadn't cared whether he had coffee or not.

In the kitchen it became very clear he didn't have any coffee or a coffeemaker. Glancing at the clock on the stove, he saw it was after nine. Had he slept all night? He never slept for more than two hours. Finding his boots, he pulled them on. He knew where to find coffee.

Going out the back door, he glanced toward the mound of fresh dirt and the pain wasn't there like before. Just an incredible gratitude that he had gotten through yesterday. And grateful that Pepper was now at peace.

Lacey should be home from taking Emma to school. Lights were on in the kitchen. He gently knocked.

"Just a minute," she called. A second later she opened the door.

At the sight of her, his mouth fell open and he quickly closed it. She was dressed in dark skinny pants and knee-high leather boots with a lime-green turtleneck sweater. Her short blond hair framed her face. For the first time he realized how beautiful and sexy she looked. How had he not seen that before?

Parts of the previous night came back to him: the fragrant scent of her hair, the softness of her skin and the gentleness of her touch. It had been a long time since he'd held a woman, and all those old urges were still alive in him. He wasn't sure how, because most of the time he had felt dead. But not today.

"Good morning," she said with a smile in her voice. "Come in."

He motioned toward her. "Obviously, you're getting ready to go out, so I won't bother you."

"I'm going to Temple to Christmas shop. That can wait for a few minutes. Would you like a cup of coffee?"

He stepped into the warm house. "That's why I came over—to bum coffee."

"You're in luck because I'm out of my Keurig cups and had to make a regular pot this morning."

He slid onto a bar stool and watched as she reached for a cup and filled it. The boots gave her height, and his eyes strayed to the roundness of her bottom and full- ness of her breasts. A new energy surged through him.

She placed the steaming mug in front of him. "Did you sleep well?"

"Yes. All night, actually, and I feel rested." He lifted the cup and took a sip.

"I'm glad."

His eyes met hers over the rim of the cup. "Sorry I unloaded on you last night. You're very good at deal- ing with grief."

"I know deep in my heart that one day Emma and I will get past it. And you will, too. They say that time heals all wounds, and I'm counting on it."

"You're a very strong lady."

She tossed her head. "Oh, please. Don't tell my irre- sponsible nature that. In Austin, I lived an easy, care- free lifestyle. Work and play—that was it. My biggest responsibility was to make sure my paycheck went into my account before I paid bills." Her green eyes grew thoughtful. "But it's strange when responsibility is thrust upon us—we either fold like a cheap tent or rise like a phoenix. I'm somewhere in between—a work in progress."

"I don't believe that for minute. In my experience, there aren't many young women who would take on the responsibility of raising a six-year-old, especially when their whole life is ahead of them."

"Didn't I tell you I'm a martyr?"

He got lost in the sparkle of her eyes, and it was the best way to start his day. This was his first step forward. He slid off the bar stool.

"I'll leave so you can do your shopping."

"Wait." She reached for a cabinet door and opened it, pulling out a thermos. "You can take the rest of the coffee."

"I have a thermos of yours I need to return."

She handed him the filled thermos. "Now you have two."

With the thermos in his hand, he knew he should say something, but looking at her his words were all jumbled with the new feelings inside him. He wasn't ready for any kind of relationship, and he had a feeling she wasn't, either. He wasn't even sure if that was what he wanted. The only thing he knew was that he liked her and she was easy to talk to, easy to be with. And right now that was the most valuable thing in his life.

He raised the thermos. "Have fun shopping."

She followed him to the door. "I ordered Emma a red bicycle with a white basket in front, and they called that it was in so I have to pick it up. I'm not sure how I'm going to hide it from her. I think I can get it into the attic."

"You can hide it in my house."

She seemed taken aback for a moment. "Oh. I wasn't hinting at…"

"I know. But I have lots of room, and it's the very least I can do for a neighbor."

"Gabe, it's… Thank you."

He tipped his head and walked out, feeling alive and taking baby steps back into a world that didn't seem so bad after all.

Chapter Nine

All the way to Temple, Lacey resisted the urge to go back. Gabe had seemed to want to talk this morning, which was so unusual for him. But last night had been a breakthrough, and she wanted to be there for him if he needed her.

The moment she thought that, she realized she was getting involved too quickly. Gabe had made it clear on more than one occasion that he'd rather be alone, and she had to respect that, just as she kept telling Emma. But she couldn't get the vulnerable man she'd held in her arms last night out of her head.

She had an appointment at the bank and she made it just in time. Her father had had a excellent life insurance policy and Lacey wouldn't have to worry about work for some time. But cleaning house and doing laundry were going to get old quickly. Once Emma didn't need her so much, Lacey would have to find something to do. In Horseshoe that would probably be difficult. For now, though, her goal was to make the best Christmas possible for Emma.

The appointment went well. She'd put a large sum of money in a trust fund for Emma's education and she had to sign papers to finalize everything. From there, she went to the mall and shopped. She bought Emma two outfits, another pair of boots, a couple of games and an iPod. The Christmas music piped into the stores put her in the mood for the holiday season. She only hoped that as Christmas drew nearer, Emma would feel the same way.

After leaving the mall, she stopped at a craft store and bought stretchy string to make bracelets for Emma's friends. Then she bought beads and ribbons, and supplies to make a wreath for the front door. She bought more than she'd planned, but it was Christmas.

Her last stop was the sporting-goods store to pick up the bicycle. She waited at customer service and was shocked when the guy brought out a box.

She looked at the ticket in her hand. "You have the wrong order. I bought a bicycle. It's red and white."

The teenage boy with a pimple on his forehead, which she tried not to look at, replied, "This is it. You have to put it together."

"What?" She had no idea how to put together a bicycle.

"No. I picked one out that was put together. It had a white basket on it."

The kid shook his head. "That's the display."

"Well, that's the one I want."

"It's not for sale," the kid said in a slow voice as if he was talking to a child. Lacey realized she might be overreacting. Evidently this was normal.

She took a deep breath and tried again. "Can someone in the store put it together? I'd be willing to pay."

The boy pulled on the earring in his ear as if he was trying to conjure up someone else to talk to her. "There's a guy here that does that, but he's pretty booked up. I'm not sure you can get it by Christmas."

This was getting her nowhere. She had to do a lot of

things with tools while decorating for parties, so surely she could put together a bicycle. If not, she'd have to ask someone for help. Maybe even Gabe. But that might be too painful for him.

"Could you please put it in my car?"

The boy sighed with obvious relief. "Yes, ma'am."

In a matter of minutes she was on her way to Horseshoe with the bicycle in the box. She had almost reached town when she noticed pine trees and the ground beneath them littered with pinecones. Two young girls about twelve were selling bags of them. Pulling over to the side of the road, she waited for the traffic to pass and then she turned around and went back. She bought three bags.

When Lacey arrived home, she carried the craft items and pinecones inside and put them in her bedroom. Then she was off to find Gabe. Her heart hummed a little faster at the thought. A loud sound echoed across her backyard, and she knew Gabe was working on something again.

She peeked out her kitchen window and couldn't believe her eyes. Gabe was at the top of the dead oak tree in his yard sawing limbs off with a chain saw. Oh, good heavens! The man was going to hurt himself. She hurried outside.

Gabe's yard was littered with dead branches. The sound of the saw was deafening. There was no way to get his attention. But just then the sound stopped. Gabe placed the saw in the crook of a branch and made his way down the tree.

His dark hair was tousled, and sweat soaked his T-shirt. She thought he'd never looked so handsome because that blank look in his eyes was gone. There was actually a light there now. A burning light that bode well for the future.

He removed his gloves. "You're back."

"And you're cutting down a tree all by yourself."

He looked at the mess in the yard. "Yep. Should keep me busy for a few days."

"Is that your goal? To always stay busy?"

He inclined his head. "Just about. How was the shopping?"

"Did you know that a bicycle comes in a box? And you have to put it together like a puzzle?"

A slight grin touched his mouth. It was the most beautiful sight she'd ever seen. It released the sad grieving man and made him irresistible.

"Yes. That's how they come."

"Well, I wish someone had told me that."

He stuffed his gloves into his back pocket. "Would it have stopped you from buying the bicycle?"

"Probably not."

"I'll help you. It's not hard if you follow the directions." He eyed her briefly and blood rushed to her face. "I have a feeling you don't follow directions too often."

She frowned. "Why do you say that?"

"The burned food, for one thing."

"Okay, you have a point." She glanced toward her house. "Can I please put the bicycle in your house? I have to pick up Emma in a few minutes, and she gets all paranoid if I'm not there exactly on time."

Lacey wound up putting all of the gifts in his spare bedroom, which was empty. The whole house was just about empty.

Gabe stared at the pile of gifts. "That's a lot for one child."

"Did you not buy a lot for Zack at Christmas?"

She thought he would shut down immediately, but he didn't. "Dana, my ex, would go overboard every year, even though we would say each time we would cut back. We never did and now I'm glad we didn't. Zack had the best Christmases." He looked away as he said the last word.

She wanted to hug him. She didn't know why she always had that feeling when she was around him. Maybe because a man who was hurting as much as he was needed lots of hugs.

He quickly recovered. "You'd better go or you'll be late."

"Oh, yes, and thanks." She ran for her car, once again feeling as though she didn't want to leave him. But Gabe was doing fine and didn't need her fussing over him.

GABE GRABBED A bottle of water out of his refrigerator and headed for his deck. He actually had bottled water because he'd gone shopping that morning after Lacey had left. He'd bought food, too, and a coffeemaker.

He stared at the mess in his yard. It would take him about a week to get it all cleaned up, and then he'd have a lot of firewood. He thought of stopping to put the bike together, but he'd rather do that with Lacey because he felt she would want to be a part of it. And she might get upset with him if he did it on his own.

Lacey was like a breath of fresh air in a world that had become dark and stale to him. For months he hadn't even known she was there. Hadn't wanted to know. He'd even cringed whenever he'd seen her and the kid outside. She'd invaded his privacy more than once, and her audacity had angered him. That same audacity had sparked a flame inside him that lit the fuse of his emotions—emotions he'd thought had died with Zack.

All day he'd been waiting for her to come home. He

didn't know why. He just liked being with her. She made the loneliness bearable. And that was saying a lot.

He heard a sound and realized it was his cell phone. Where was it? He followed the sound into the kitchen and saw it on the counter. It was his sister. Most of the time he just ignored it, but today he clicked on.

"Hi, sis."

"You answered."

"Sorry about the other times." He sat at the kitchen table. "I just wasn't in the mood to talk."

"I worry about you."

"I know, but I told you I needed my space."

"So what's different now?"

He told her about Pepper and Lacey and Emma.

"That's Jack Carroll's family?"

"Yes. Emma was very fond of Pepper."

"I'm glad they were there for you, but if you had called I would've been there."

"Kate, don't mother me. You have seven sons for that."

"Like any of them listen to me."

"Oh, they listen."

Kate chuckled. "So tell me about this Lacey. Is she raising the little girl?"

"Yes." The question was an awakening moment. He knew nothing about Lacey's personal life other than she was raising her sister.

"How old is she?"

"Kate, stop with the inquisition. I know very little about her because I value my privacy."

"Oh, please don't start that again."

"And that's the reason I don't answer my phone most of the time. You treat me like one of your sons."

"Okay, I get it. But please come out to the ranch for supper one night. We'd all love to see you."

"I'm not making any promises, but I'll think about it."

"I just want you to be happy again."

Gabe didn't know if that was possible. "Bye, sis."

He walked out to his deck, his head filled with thoughts of Lacey. Taking a seat, he knew he was having a surreal moment, which wasn't unusual. He had those daily. This was different, though. He'd leaned on someone for the first time in his life, and he knew little about her except that she was kind, compassionate, understanding and selfless. She wasn't like anyone he'd ever known. And he was thinking too much about her. He drank the last of his water and went back to work, but thoughts of Lacey lingered.

WHEN LACEY ARRIVED at school Emma wasn't there waiting. Lacey got out and looked around. A moment of panic ran through her until she saw a group of kids. She started over and Emma broke away and ran toward her.

The first thing Lacey noticed was the fear on Emma's face. Second, the headband and bow Lacey had made were gone from Emma's hair.

Lacey hugged her and asked, "Did school let out early?"

Emma shrugged. "We had a program and when it was over, they said we could go home. And you weren't here." Her bottom lip trembled.

"I didn't know you were getting out early."

Emma had been very afraid Lacey was going to leave her. Lacey had done everything to reassure her that she wasn't, but Emma's fears were very real.

"I will always be here, sweetie. Please remember that."

Emma hiccupped. "'Kay."

"What happened to your bow?" Lacey asked as they got into the car.

"I gave it to Bailey."

"Why?"

"She gave me something, so I gave her something. You can make me another and she liked my bow."

"Sweetie, I don't want you giving away your stuff."

"But…" Lacey looked in the rearview mirror and saw Emma's bottom lip tremble again.

Oh, good heavens. Lacey had wanted Emma to make friends and now Lacey was spoiling it. She couldn't have it both ways.

"It's okay, sweetie. I'll make you another. Now let's go to the bakery and get a snack."

The scent in the bakery was decadent. Lacey could gain five pounds just from the smell.

"Hey, cutie," Angie's sister, AnaMarie, said from behind the counter. "I missed you yesterday."

It was an opening line for Emma to talk about Pepper. AnaMarie listened avidly as she prepared Emma's cherry kolach and hot chocolate.

"Sweetie, I'm going to speak to Angie for second. I'll be right back." Lacey went down the hall to Angie's office. Angie was an accountant. She did just about everyone's taxes in Horseshoe, and she did the bakery's books.

Lacey tapped on the door frame. "Are you busy?

Angie glanced up. "Well, look at you. All dressed up. What's the occasion?"

Lacey took the chair across from Angie. "I had to go into Temple today, so I made an effort with my appearance. I'll be back in jeans tomorrow."

Angie leaned back in her chair. "Cooking lessons and dressing up. I get the feeling it's for someone special."

"I wish." Lacey couldn't believe she squirmed in her

chair like a teenager. "I have to admit, though, the sandwiches were for my next-door neighbor."

"You mean Gabe Garrison?"

"Yes. I just wanted to lift his spirits a little. I'm hopeless in the kitchen, so I don't know what I was thinking."

"It's so sad about his little boy."

"Mmm. And he had to put his son's dog to sleep."

"Oh, no. We've all tried to reach out to him, but he's made it very clear he values his privacy. Hardy knows him and so does Wyatt. He attended Horseshoe schools. He's a couple years younger, I think. I vaguely remember him. Very handsome with a brilliant future ahead of him."

"My dad had mentioned he was from here."

"Is Gabe doing okay?"

"It's hard to tell, but I think he's getting better. At least he's friendlier. And that brings me to my next question."

Angie smiled. "I can almost guess."

"I want to cook a really good meal. Believe me, the man could use it. So can you tell me how to do a roast the simple way?"

Angie pulled a pad and pencil forward. "I'll write it down step by step."

The front door opened and Peyton Carson, her two-year-old son, J.W., her daughter, Jody, and Erin came in. Jody and Erin were inseparable and best friends.

"One daughter delivered safe and sound," Peyton said. Peyton was a beautiful blonde who caught everyone's eye.

"Hi, Mama." Erin kissed her mother.

J.W. ran through to the kitchen. "Jody, get him," Peyton said to her daughter. Looking over Angie's shoulder, she asked, "What are you doing?"

"Writing out a recipe for Lacey."

Peyton held up two fingers. "I have two words for you. Crock-Pot. Or is that one word?" She shook her head. "Doesn't matter. You just throw everything in there and let it cook. Simple. Wyatt actually thinks I'm a good cook and I'm never telling him differently."

"That's the lazy way of cooking," Angie told her.

"Don't listen to her." Peyton laughed. "She cooks everything the hard way. Really. I mean who does that? No one but Angie."

The two were best friends, and Lacey knew they were teasing each other.

Angie handed Lacey the recipe. "Text or call me if you have a problem."

"Thanks." Lacey rose to her feet. "I better get Emma and go home. It's been a long day and I'm ready to get out of these boots."

"Crock-Pot," Peyton called as Lacey walked out of the bakery.

Lacey smiled. It was nice to be around women near her age. She missed that connection she had in Austin. Every day life seemed to get a little better. She still had Christmas and Emma to worry about, but she was going to cook Gabe a delicious meal whether he wanted it or not. She might burn the house down doing it. The smoke alarm would save her, though. God bless that annoying little piece of technology. But who would save her from Gabe and her growing feelings for him?

Chapter Ten

The next morning after dropping Emma at school, Lacey went to the supermarket. She'd seen Angie at the school and Angie had given her more cooking advice. Angie had said the man at the meat counter could help Lacey select a roast. He did, and she took what he suggested. Emma liked mashed potatoes, so Lacey bought potatoes and a peeler. She was set for a day of cooking.

As she unpacked groceries, she could hear Gabe's saw. It had been buzzing until late the previous night. He was determined to finish the tree.

Lacey laid out Angie's instructions on the counter and went to work. With the roast browned on one side, she flipped it over to brown the other. Her cell buzzed and she fished it out of her purse. It was Janine, her former boss.

"Hey, Janine." Lacey went into the living room and sat on the sofa.

"How are things going?"

"Pretty good. I have a roast in the oven."

Janine laughed. "You're getting domesticated."

"We have to eat, so I'm trying to learn."

"Why not come back to work and pay someone to cook?"

"I wish I could, but there's no way I can leave Emma.

I have to be here when she gets out of school. Besides, the drive every day would kill me."

"Have you thought of moving back to Austin? We have a lot of good schools here, and you and Emma could start over."

The thought was so tempting, but she pushed it aside because it wasn't really what she wanted. "This is Emma's home, and I don't know how she would react to leaving all the memories of our dad. She's still grieving." *And so am I.*

Janine sighed. "I gave it a shot. We're so busy with the holiday season, and I could really use your help."

"Sorry. I'm dealing with a little girl who doesn't believe in Santa Claus, and that takes all my energy." Lacey told her what had happened.

"I'm sorry, Lacey. I know you have your hands full, but remember to have some fun for yourself."

The smoke alarm shrilled and Lacey jumped to her feet. "I gotta go. I'll call you later."

She threw the phone on the sofa and ran. The kitchen was filling up with smoke coming from the oven. Damn! The shrilling sound jabbed like sharp needles at her brain. She quickly turned off the oven and then removed her sneaker and threw it at the pesky thing. The alarm flew off and landed in the dining room. She picked it up and threw it out the back door. Opening the oven door, she coughed as smoke billowed out into the kitchen and dining room. Damn! Her dinner was ruined. What was she thinking? She couldn't cook. She sank to her knees, slapped away an errant tear and had her own private pity party.

GABE WAS GOING into his house for water when he heard the alarm. Not again. What was she doing? Unable to resist, he strolled over. As he neared her back door, the smoke alarm landed at his feet. He retrieved it from the dry winter grass and then opened the door. Smoke engulfed him.

He covered his mouth. "Lacey, are you okay?" He saw her sitting on the floor and went to her. "Lacey?"

"I burned my beautiful roast," she mumbled. "It's black. What's wrong with me that I can't cook?"

"Is it just the roast? Nothing else is on fire?"

She nodded and he took her arm and helped her to her feet. "Let's get out of here until the smoke clears."

As she limped toward the back door, he realized she had on one sneaker. Searching the kitchen, he found the other one on the counter. He opened the kitchen window and followed her out the door.

After taking a seat at her patio table, he handed her the sneaker and she slipped it on. She ran her fingers through her short hair and fluffed it. Even with tear trails on her face, she looked beautiful.

"I'm hopeless."

"Have you never cooked?"

Her eyes narrowed, and he was expecting a whole lot of attitude, but she replied, "Not really."

"Why?"

The eyes narrowed even more. "Don't push your luck. I'm not in a good mood."

"I'm just asking a question."

"I liked it better when you were quiet."

He leaned forward. "I know very little about you. Is your mother still living?"

She laughed, a bubbly sound that lifted his spirits.

"What's so funny?"

She pointed a finger at him. "You wanting to talk."

Their eyes met, and he felt a chink in that solid armor

he'd built around his heart. To avoid further analysis, he asked, "Any brothers or sisters?"

She shook her head. "I was an only child until Emma."

"A spoiled, pampered child?"

She closed her eyes as if giving it some thought. "Yes, mainly by my father. My mother worked a lot and still does."

"It must have changed your world when Emma came along."

She tucked her feet beneath her. "Not really. I wasn't as spoiled as you might think. The thought of having a sister was exciting, and I loved her the moment I saw her. I couldn't wait to leave work and come see her. And Mona was very good about letting me visit any time I wanted."

"That was your stepmom?"

"Yes."

She rubbed her jeans absently. "She only lived for six months after Emma was born, and I think she leaned on me a lot to care for Emma. Dad did, too. He had his hands full taking care of Mona. It was so sad. My dad deserved happiness, not what he got." She brushed away a tear and Gabe's stomach clenched. He wanted to take away her pain just as she had tried to take away his.

Before he could say anything, she continued, "My parents had a lousy marriage. They argued all the time. After nineteen years, my mom told my dad to leave and he did. It shocked her, I think. Anyway—" she waved a hand "—it was a bitter divorce and I was caught in the middle. My mother wanted me to hate my dad and I couldn't. Now she wants me to hate Emma, and I can't do that, either. Suffice to say, Mom and I are always at odds. I love her, but it's hard dealing with her."

"Where does your mother live?" He was caught off

guard by the words coming out of his mouth, but he found he was curious about her.

"In Austin. She got our family home in the divorce. She wants me to come home for Christmas, but she doesn't want me to bring Emma. That's causing a lot of friction, because I can't leave Emma."

He'd never met anyone quite like Lacey. She had sacrificed her chance at a life so a little girl could have a home. The more he talked to her, the more he admired her.

"I'm sure it will work out."

"You don't know my mother."

If she was that hard-hearted, Gabe didn't want to know the woman. But then, he wasn't in the mood to associate with many people. Lacey was an exception.

"So your mom didn't cook?"

Lacey smiled a smile that rivaled the sun, and for moment he was lost in her charm. "Getting back to the cooking, huh? No, she doesn't cook. My dad did all the cooking. Sometimes I would help, but he did all the major stuff. I just played. He was an awesome dad. I don't know why he thought I would make a good mother for Emma. I'm terrible at it. Every day I feel like a failure."

"Every parent feels that way. You never know if you're doing the right thing. You just have to trust your instincts and your heart. When Za…" Gabe caught himself in time. He couldn't talk about his son.

She looked up. "What about Zack?" He should've known she wouldn't leave it alone.

"Nothing," he replied sharply, hoping she got the message.

She stared at him, her green eyes soft and understanding, as if she knew what he was thinking, and she was urging him toward something he didn't want but desperately needed.

Before he knew it, words tumbled from his throat. "When Zack would misbehave, my wife, Dana, always expected me to be the disciplinarian. And it killed me. I hated that part of being a parent. I guess if I had been sterner and not so lenient, Zack wouldn't have..." He drew a deep breath and knew he had to say the words. He couldn't just think them. "Za...Zack wouldn't have disobeyed." A wad of guilt burned his throat.

"What did Zack do?" she asked softly.

Gabe focused on a terra-cotta pot on the patio table. "When we got the four-wheeler, we sat down and made rules. Zack could only ride it on weekends when I was home. During the week he had homework and school activities. He agreed and I trusted him. I put the key in my nightstand." Gabe drew another breath. "Dana always picked him up from school. She was doing some legal work for one of our neighbors. She left Zack to do homework and drove to their house to leave papers. When she returned, she couldn't find Zack. She immediately called me and I came home. He'd found the key and had taken the four-wheeler for a spin. He'd turned it over, and I found him with the vehicle on top of him. His chest was crushed and...I pulled it off and carried him to the house. An ambulance was on the way...but it was too late. My son...was dead."

Lacey slipped onto his lap and wrapped her arms around his neck. "I'm so sorry."

He sucked air into his tight lungs. "I think we've done this before."

"You're talking about it, and that's good. It doesn't help to keep it all bottled up inside."

Her hand stroked his neck, and he lost his train of

thought. The pain inside him ebbed and new, vibrant feelings emerged. She smelled of smoke mixed with a flowery scent that was all woman—a delicate fragrance that filled his nostrils and awakened needs deep inside him. His hand rested on the curve of her hip, and the urge was strong to move upward to her breasts, to feel their fullness.

"The smoke has cleared," he said, getting to his feet. He needed to put distance between them. "Let's check out the damage."

She followed him inside. "This is my last attempt at cooking. From now on, we're eating sandwiches."

He opened the oven door. "You don't seem like a person who gives up that easily."

"How many times have you heard the smoke alarm?"

"Point taken." He found a hot pad on the counter and lifted the pan out of the oven. Inside was a charred lump of meat. "How long have you been cooking this thing?"

"Not long."

He placed the pan on another hot pad. "This is really burned. Maybe there's something wrong with your oven."

She smacked her forehead with the palm of her hand and he wanted to laugh, which felt good. "The oven. Why didn't I think of that? Please let it be the oven."

He closed the door and set the dial to two hundred degrees. They both stared through the little glass window. It was an electric stove, and the coils became red instantly. "Whoa. It's heating up fast. That's not normal. The thermostat must be broken."

"Really?" Her voice rose with excitement. "Could that be the problem?"

"These houses were built about twenty years ago, and this is probably the original oven. A repair guy will cost a lot of money. It might be best to just replace the built-in oven."

"This was Mona's house, and when she married my dad, he replaced the floors, painted and did some updating. I don't think he replaced the appliances. Maybe I'll just buy a new one, but I'll have to get someone to install it."

"I'll do it," he offered. "If you're free in the morning we can go to Temple and pick out a new one. I'll measure it so we can get the right size to fit."

"Thank you." She reached up and hugged him, and he tensed. He couldn't help that reaction. His feelings were all over the place and he had to take a step back. He didn't want to cause either of them any more problems.

"Where's your ladder? I'll put the smoke alarm back up."

"In the garage."

It didn't take him long to reinstall the alarm. He carried the ladder back to the garage and made his getaway.

He felt like a coward, running away, but that was all he could do at the moment. Lacey was too nice for him to hurt and he'd realized recently that soon he'd have to return to his old life. When that would happen, he wasn't quite sure. Right now, he was enjoying the crazy lady next door.

LACEY HURRIED TO pick up Emma. As soon as Emma walked into the house, she said, "Not again, Lacey. What did you burn?"

"It wasn't my fault. We need a new oven."

"You're blaming the oven?"

"Yes, smarty-pants, Gabe said the thermostat is broken."

Emma threw her backpack on the sofa. "I'm gonna

go see Gabe." Lately, Emma had dropped the *Mr.* from Gabe's name, and Lacey saw no need to correct her. Emma and Gabe were now friends.

"Wait a minute. Gabe is busy working on the tree and you might be in the way."

"I want to see if my flowers are still on Pepper's grave."

"Just stay a minute because you have homework to do."

"'Kay."

Emma shot out the door, and Lacey resisted the impulse to go with her. She wanted to see Gabe, too. But she'd sensed his withdrawal from her. She should give him his space. They were drawing closer and it was making him nervous. It made her a little nervous, too, but she found it exciting at the same time.

The evening went as usual. Emma complained about homework and about washing her hair, but eventually Lacey got her into bed. The morning came quickly. She dropped Emma at school and hurried home.

As soon as she pulled into the driveway, Gabe came over with a measuring tape. He got the serial number and make off the door, and then they were on their way to Temple. He insisted on going in his truck. She got the impression he didn't trust her driving.

The truck was nice, with heated leather seats. In his other life, she realized he must've had money. As he was a lawyer, she could understand that.

"You can do a lot of things," she remarked.

"I was raised with seven nephews, and my brother-in-law made sure we knew how to survive in this world."

"What happened to your parents?"

She expected him to clam up, but he didn't. "My dad left soon after I was born. He was a truck driver and traveled all over the States. He met my mom when he was passing through Horseshoe. Settling down wasn't his thing. I met him for the first time about five years ago. I tracked him down. He had remarried three times after my mom. I was his only child, though. He lives on the Gulf Coast, fishing, these days. Even after all this time, he still wasn't interested in being a father. We parted amicably."

How sad, Lacey thought. "And your mom?"

He shifted uneasily in his seat. "She died when I was fourteen. I have a half sister who is eighteen years older than me, and instead of seeing me put into foster care, she insisted I live with her and her family. She and her husband, John, already had seven sons, and they accepted me as one of them."

"Seven sons?" Lacey tried to keep the awe out of her voice, but failed.

"Yeah, seven rambunctious boys in about eight years. Two were born in the same year. Jude was born in January and Phoenix in December."

"Where do they live?"

"On a ranch not far out of Horseshoe."

"And they never visit you?" That question might have been out of line, but she couldn't take it back.

His hands gripped the wheel, his eyes glued to the highway. "I told them not to. I needed my space and they respected my wishes." He zoomed around a car that he obviously thought was going too slow. "At least my nephews have. My sister, Kate, hasn't been quite as accommodating. She tends to treat me like one of her boys."

Kate. "Kate Rebel?"

He glanced at her. "You know my sister?"

"Um…" She should have kept her mouth shut. Now she had to tell him what she'd done. "No, not really.

The day the vet came to put Pepper to sleep, I used your phone to call the school about Emma. I was going to ask you, but you were busy with the vet. I didn't think you'd mind one phone call. I just happened to see all the missed calls from Kate Rebel."

He spared her another sharp glance. "You used my phone without permission. Do you even know what the word *privacy* means?"

His reprimanding tone needled her. "Okay. I did it. I'm sorry. Spank me."

The corners of his mouth twitched. "Do you know you're a little crazy?"

"Yep. And lovable."

"And infuriating."

"But you like me."

His eyes met hers. "Yes. I like you."

That was more than she'd ever thought she would hear from him. And it was enough.

Chapter Eleven

Shopping with Lacey was like nothing Gabe had ever experienced. She looked at all the ovens, even the ones that wouldn't fit her space. Grabbing her attention to focus on what she needed was like catching dust motes in his hand. Impossible. Then, after looking for more than an hour, she decided she didn't like any of them. At the third store, he'd had enough.

"This is it," he told her. "You're picking out an oven that will fit your kitchen and we're not looking at ones that will not."

"Maybe," she said, sliding out of the truck.

He groaned, but followed her inside. He found one that was almost the exact measurements and showed it to her.

"This will do. The measurements are an eighth of an inch off, but I can make it work."

She pointed to one farther down the aisle. "I like that one."

He counted to three. "It's a double oven. You have a single oven."

"Okay. Don't get testy."

He bit his lip. "See. This one has a timer and push buttons. Easy to use."

"I like that."

"Good." He motioned to the salesman. "We'll take it."
He waited for her to object, but she didn't. They bought
the oven and were soon on their way back to Horseshoe.

"Let's get an ice cream."

"No," he replied. "I can have the oven in by this afternoon."

She turned in her seat to face him. "There's no rush.
You can do it tomorrow or the next day. I'm not exactly
Rachael Ray tied to the stove. You need to lighten up
and have some fun."

"I don't know what having fun is like anymore."

"I'll show you." She pointed to a Dairy Queen up
ahead. "Pull in."

"No. We can be home in no time."

"Pull in."

He pulled in. Rolling into the drive-through, he
pushed a button to lower his window. She leaned across
him and said to the young girl, "Two medium ice cream
cones, dipped."

"I don't want one."

"He does," Lacey stated, but the girl hesitated. "He
does," she repeated, and the young girl turned to make
them.

He was fighting a losing battle, so he gave in. He took
the cones and handed them to Lacey while he paid the
girl. "I can't drive eating ice cream."

"Oh, my, the man who can do everything can't eat
ice cream and drive."

"It's not safe."

"Then find a spot and we'll eat them here."

He found a parking space and turned off the engine.
She handed him a cone and he ate it like a good little
boy. There was blissful silence for a change.

After wiping her mouth, she placed the napkin on the

console and turned his rearview mirror toward her. He gritted his teeth.

"There's a mirror on your sun visor."

"Oh. You should have said something."

"You never give me a chance."

She made a face at him, and then turned to look in the mirror. "My lipstick is all gone. Kiss me."

"What?"

"Kissing will make my lips red. Don't you know that?"

"I…"

She caught the front of his sweatshirt and pulled him forward, planting a kiss smack on his lips. For a moment he was caught off guard, but found his lips responding in the most sensual way.

Pulling back, she licked her lips. "Cool and chocolaty. Nice." She puckered her lips. "Are they pink?"

His lips cracked into a smile. He couldn't help himself. She was infectious and tempting and drawing him in with her delightful personality.

"You are crazy."

"See?" She touched his lips with one finger, and he wanted to grab it with his teeth and nibble and… "I made you smile. It helps to be a little crazy and not to take life so seriously." She glanced at her watch. "Oh, we have to hurry. I can't be late for picking up Emma."

It amazed him how she could go from fun loving to responsible. He started the truck, and once again they were on their way home. Gabe felt something different, unusual and welcoming. A sliver of light opened in his heart. He could feel it—warm and comfortable, like sunshine, filling his system with much-needed nourishment. And at that moment he realized he needed a little crazy in his life.

LACEY WAS THERE when Emma got out of school, and they went to the bakery for a snack. She thought she'd give Gabe some time to do what he had to in the kitchen. With her and Emma underfoot, he'd be scowling the whole time. Much like he had been today.

She'd been silly on purpose to draw him out of his serious mood, which he always seemed to be in. And it had worked. He'd smiled for the first time. It was breathtaking to see the change on his face. He'd allowed himself to feel something other than pain. If she had to be silly to accomplish that, then so be it.

At the bakery, Angie laughed about the burned roast, but was glad to hear it was the oven's fault. Lacey bought kolaches to take home for dessert. Emma was all excited when Lacey told her Gabe was putting in a new oven. She could hardly wait to charge into the house.

Lacey was surprised to see Gabe was almost finished. With some kind of tool, he was tightening the screws to the cabinet.

He wiped a rag over the front of the new appliance. "All done."

"We have a new oven. Now Lacey won't burn our food," Emma said.

Gabe put his tools back into a toolbox. "There's some sawdust on the floor. I had to shave off some wood to make it fit, but the lip on the oven covers it."

"I'll sweep it up." Lacey went to get the broom out of the utility room.

"The old one is on the patio," Gabe told her. "I'll haul it to the dump in the morning."

She tilted her head. "Thank you, kind sir. And for your reward we're having fish sticks, macaroni and cheese and kolaches for supper. You're invited to stay."

"Thanks, but I'm not really hungry."

"You'll come anyway." Her eyes held his, and for a moment she thought he was going to refuse again.

"Okay, but I want to work on the tree for a while."

"Deal."

He paused at the door with the toolbox in his hand. "You know, it's getting very hard to say no to you."

"Let's keep it that way."

A smile touched his face, and it was so beautiful. It softened those hard lines that were etched by pain and suffering and made him attractive and appealing. Maybe a little too much for her peace of mind. She liked Gabe, but they really had no future. He would soon get his life together. He was already taking steps in that direction, and she would stay here in Horseshoe and raise Emma. There was nothing wrong with them being friends, though. Yet her heart wanted so much more.

"Lacey, did you make my bow?"

Emma's question brought her back to reality. "No. I haven't had time."

"Bailey and I are dressing alike tomorrow and I have to have it."

"Really?" She stared down at Emma, who obviously thought she could pull rabbits out of hats. Or would that be bows? "You could have told me that earlier."

"I did. I told you I needed another bow."

"Okay. I'll do it tonight. Start on your homework and I'll get supper started."

"I want to help Gabe."

"Not tonight. Gabe is busy."

"You're no fun, Lacey." Emma stomped to the table and crawled onto a chair.

"I'll have you know I'm lots of fun." With the broom as a prop she started twerking, twisting her arms and legs in a spastic sort of way. Turning around, she saw

Gabe standing in the doorway with a stunned expression on his face.

"Oh."

"Lacey's being silly." Emma came to the rescue.

"I thought she was having a seizure."

Emma laughed and Lacey frowned.

"I just wanted to tell you that I'm taking the old oven and putting it in the back of my truck. I had no idea I was in for a show."

"Lacey's weird." Emma pulled books out of her backpack.

Lacey lifted an eyebrow, daring him to say one word.

"Hmm." He walked out, and she sank back against the counter. After a moment, she recovered and started supper.

Gabe came over and ate with them, as promised, but he didn't stay long.

That night Lacey made the bow, and the next day Emma and Bailey marched into the school dressed alike in their candy cane outfits. They looked adorable.

Lacey didn't dawdle, though. Since Gabe had helped her yesterday, she planned to return the favor. He had the tree completely cut down—only a stump remained, but branches were strewn all over his yard. He was cutting the branches into firewood.

"Good morning," he said, turning off the chain saw. "Where do you want the wood stacked? I'll help."

"You don't have to do that."

"And you didn't have to install my oven, so let's don't argue. Where do you want me to stack the logs?"

He pointed to a place near the house where he had already started a pile. They worked in silence, except for the chain saw. She paused every now and then to watch him. Since the sun was out, he'd removed his hoodie.

His black T-shirt emphasized the muscles in his arms. He'd put on a little weight and he looked damn good.

His cowboy boots were worn and dirty and his long hair dripped with sweat. Masculinity with a capital *M*. She had never been more aware of it than she was today.

Lacey was exhausted by the time she had to pick up Emma, but Gabe's yard looked a little better. There were still branches and debris everywhere, but most of the big branches had been cut up and stacked.

She had a few minutes before she had to leave, so they sat on his deck, drinking water. The weather was beautiful—sunny and in the sixties. A slight breeze ruffled her hair, and she felt relaxed just sitting there with him. She wondered if he felt the same way.

"What are you gonna do with all this wood?"

"Burn it in the fireplace when it gets colder. You and Emma can come over and I'll make s'mores."

"You're inviting us over?"

"Why not?"

"Exactly." She placed her bottle on the floor. "I'm going to try to get Emma to decorate the tree this weekend."

"Just take it slow and don't force her."

"That's what all the books say, and I've read just about every one, but it's so frustrating. I want her to believe and to feel the excitement of Christmas like I did as a child. I want her to have good memories. I want her to be a little girl with stardust in her eyes."

"What does Emma want?"

"What?"

"You keep saying what you want. Ask Emma how she wants to celebrate Christmas. Give her a chance to express her feelings and gradually pull her in. I know you can do that because you're constantly pulling me in to things I don't want to do."

She placed her hands on her hips. "Like what?"

He took a big swig from the water bottle. "Like… making me smile and making me realize that I'm still alive."

"Poor you."

"Yeah, poor me."

She wasn't offended by his words because there was a slight smile on his lips. And she loved it—loved that he was finally letting go of all the pain. Little by little he was getting better. But when he reached the pinnacle of full recovery, would he still hang around Horseshoe, Texas?

GABE NEVER KNEW what to expect from Lacey. That was part of her charm. She was now in full Christmas mode and totally involved with cooking. Whenever he'd go over to her house, she was either watching cooking shows on TV or reading recipes on the internet. Every night she made something different and he ate with them. She was getting good, and it wasn't hard to get caught up in her excitement.

If she wasn't trying a recipe, she was decorating or making pinecone wreaths for the door and the fireplace. He'd helped hold the cones so she could tie them in place on a rounded wire. And he'd helped hold the red plaid ribbon she then wove through the pinecones. She'd added red berries for an extra touch.

She was very good at crafts. There were now a lot of decorations for Emma to put on the tree, but it wasn't working. The tree still stood, looking lonely and bare, in the living room.

As he returned from his morning jog, he noticed

Lacey on the ladder in the front yard nailing Christmas lights to the house. He watched her for a moment, enjoying the view. She wore tight-fitting jeans and a knit top that showed off her figure to perfection. And he was happy to recognize that he found her curves enticing.

He walked up to her. "What are you doing?"

She looked down at him. "Uh…it's not hard to figure out. I'm going to light this house up like Cowboy Stadium. Emma has to get in the Christmas mood soon."

"I could say you're crazy, but I think I've covered that."

"Yes. Crazy like a fox. I have no idea what that means, but I've heard it all my life."

He didn't feel the need to enlighten her. Lacey was just Lacey—charming.

"The wind is picking up. You need to get down from there before you break your neck."

"Oh, please. This is what I did in my job. Hang decorations for ladies who wanted everything just right. Believe me, when you have to hang decorations in a ballroom, it takes a tall ladder and a steady hand."

"I thought you were an assistant."

"Yes. The person who does things when an employee doesn't show up for work. The party must go on, you know."

"I had no idea. All I know is you're too high in the air for my peace of mind."

"I'm not getting down until I finish."

"I'll go get my ladder and help you."

"Ah, a man after my heart."

For the next hour they used a staple gun to secure lights all over the front of the house. It really was going to light up the night. But then, Lacey could do that with just her smile. She scurried down the ladder to turn them on and they gazed at their handiwork.

Lacey clapped her hands. "Oh, Emma has to be excited about this."

"Yeah. Planes are going to mistake your roof for the Austin airport."

She poked him in the ribs playfully. "How about some coffee?"

"You read my mind."

He was very comfortable in Lacey's house. The more time he spent there the more he wanted to come back. Lacey's cheerful personality was inviting, and he needed that in his life right now.

He sat at her table and she placed a steaming mug of coffee and a plate of something chocolaty in front of him.

"It's fudge. I made it last night. Taste it."

"Am I a guinea pig?"

She took a seat with a gleam in her eyes. "Maybe."

"Mmm," he mumbled, munching on the sweet treat. "You're getting this cooking thing down."

Her eyes twinkled even more. "Thank you very much. Now, if I could just get Emma to believe in Santa again…"

"You have about three weeks before the kids at school will get excited and she will, too. You just have to give her time and don't push, but I don't think you hear me when I say that."

Lacey fiddled with her cup. "I try, but I don't know. Emma's very adamant. She's lost her father and now Santa has been taken from her. I can sense her stubbornness and anger, and I worry about that."

"Anger is not a good thing to live with. After Zack died, I was filled with rage. I took a hammer and beat that four-wheeler into a million pieces. Even that didn't stop the fury building in me. I snapped at everyone, and when I almost hit one of my colleagues for laughing in my presence, I knew I had to get away. I threw some things in a bag and started driving. The next thing I knew I was in Horseshoe."

He took a breath, hardly believing he was sharing that awful time.

"Did you tell your wife?"

He ran his finger over the handle of the cup. "Two weeks after the accident she moved in with her brother and his wife. She blamed me and I blamed her, but our marriage had fallen apart long before the accident. She was busy building her career and so was I. Zack was our only common interest."

"I'm sorry."

"See." He slapped his hand on the table, jarring the coffee in his cup. "You have me talking even when I don't want to."

"You do want to talk. That's why you're doing it. And it's long overdue."

"I suppose," he admitted, and wondered why it was so easy to talk to her.

"Did you come to Horseshoe to visit your sister?"

"I guess that was my destination, but I wasn't thinking about it consciously. Turns out I wasn't ready for all her smothering and sympathy. I love her, but I just couldn't handle it at that time. I slept in my truck until I saw a house for sale. I made the deal and the next day I moved in. The sofa and table were already here, and that was all furniture I needed. The sofa was my bed for a long time until I finally broke down and bought a mattress for the old iron bed in the bedroom."

She reached out and clasped his hand on the table. Her

hand was so fragile compared to his, or at least it looked that way. Fragility disguising an enormous strength.

"I'm so happy you're doing better."

"Yeah." He entwined his fingers with hers, her softness soothing against his calluses. "You're there for me and Emma. Who's there for you?"

Her green eyes clouded for a moment. "The people of Horseshoe have been very nice to us."

"How about your mother?"

"She was angry that I had accepted the responsibility of Emma and tried to persuade me to send her to Mona's sister in Midland. I couldn't do that, so I handled it alone. When dad died, Emma and I came home and we sat in his recliner and fell asleep. We stayed there the whole night. She cried. I cried. She clung to me like a leech and was afraid for me to get out of her sight. The following weeks were really hard trying to hold it together. But time moved on and people came by and brought food, visited and offered their condolences. We made it. But we're not quite there yet."

"You're amazing. Do you know that?" A smile curved her lips, and he watched it transform her into a beautiful, irresistible woman.

"And a little crazy?"

"I'm beginning to really like crazy."

Silence stretched, but it wasn't uncomfortable. It was that of two people dealing with their emotions and enjoying the moment of having someone who understood. Someone who cared.

Chapter Twelve

Lacey could hardly wait for Emma to see the house. She'd turned on the lights before she left so Emma would see them as they drove up.

For the school Christmas program, the first graders were going to sing carols. Today was their first practice, and she'd thought Emma would be all excited because she loved to sing. But when she got into the car, she was somber and quiet. Lacey asked her a few questions but then stopped. Emma was clearly annoyed about something. The house would cheer her up, Lacey was sure.

Emma crawled out of the car and then stopped as she saw the lights. Her face scrunched into her trademark frown.

"What'd you do that for?"

Lacey unlocked the front door. "Because it's Christmas and Santa has to be able to see our house."

"There is no Santa, Lacey. Sometimes you make me mad."

Lacey bent down to her level. "Sometimes you make me mad, too. So there."

"Daddy puts the lights on the house. And you're not Daddy." Emma shot toward her bedroom, the backpack in her hand.

Lacey's heart took a jolt. She'd screwed up. She sank

onto the sofa and buried her face in her hands. Gabe had told her to take it slow and not to force Emma. She should have listened. After a moment, she walked down the hall to Emma's room. Emma lay curled into a fetal position, the backpack still looped around her arm. She faced the wall, away from Lacey.

Needing time, Lacey went to her room, pulled out a couple of parenting books and tried to figure out how to make this right again. The message was clear: never force a child, be patient, be understanding, be supportive, ask their opinion, let them share their feelings, love them and let them know you love them.

She laid the book on the bed. Gabe was right. Lacey was doing what she wanted, not what Emma wanted. Damn! How could she have screwed this up so badly? She took a deep breath and went to Emma. As she removed the backpack from Emma's arm, Emma turned over. Her face was blotchy and her eyes were red from crying. Lacey could hardly stand it. She willed herself not to cry. But hurting Emma took a toll on her.

"I know I'm not Daddy, but I'm doing the best I can."

Emma flew into her, wrapping her arms around Lacey's waist and crying into her chest. "I'm…sorry I was mean to you. I'm sorry…"

"Shh." Lacey stroked Emma's hair and then lifted her sister into her arms. She sat on the bed with Emma in her lap. "It's okay. Stop crying."

Finally, Emma's wails ebbed.

As Lacey held her sister, it occurred to her that Emma's reaction was over the top. When Lacey had gotten the tree and put up the wreaths and other decorations in the house, Emma had complained, but not paid much attention to what Lacey was doing. Today was different. She thought about Emma's reluctance to talk earlier.

"Sweetie." Lacey brushed hair away from Emma's face and removed the bow that was hanging loose. "Did something happen in school today?"

Emma rubbed her face against Lacey shirt. "No. Why?"

"You're very upset."

Emma played with Lacey's watch. "I told Bailey about Pepper and Daddy, and that I sent Daddy a message with Pepper when she went to heaven, and Bailey said—" Emma hiccupped "—she said…that dogs can't talk and Pepper couldn't give Daddy my message. Now Daddy doesn't know I love him." Emma buried her face in Lacey's chest and sobbed.

So that was it. Unknowingly, Bailey had taken away Emma's happiness. Lacey reached for Emma's chin and pulled up her face.

"Daddy, Pepper and Zack are in heaven, and heaven is a beautiful place where everything is perfect. There's only one voice, whether it's a person or an animal, and it's understood by everyone. Pepper's probably licked Daddy's face, his hands and his feet in excitement to give him your message. Daddy knows, sweetie. He knows. Don't let anyone ever tell you different. You tell them to talk to your big sister, and I will set them straight."

Emma sat up, her eyes like big shiny marbles. "They're in heaven."

"Yes."

"Oh." Emma threw her arms around Lacey's neck. "I love you."

Lacey's heart melted into a drippy mess. "Love you, too, sweetie. Please talk to me when you have a problem, or when someone tells you something you don't understand or when you're just sad."

"'Kay."

"Now I'm going to fix supper. Wash your face and then you can go tell Gabe supper will be ready in a few minutes."

Emma jumped off her lap and ran to the bathroom. Lacey made her way to the kitchen, feeling a little better. Actually, she felt a lot better. Finally, she was getting this parenting thing down—at least until the next crisis.

GABE PULLED OFF his gloves. A couple more days and he'd have the backyard clean again. Emma came through the gate and jumped up the steps on the deck, and then slid into a chair.

"Hi, Gabe."

"Hi, kiddo." He sat in the other chair and waited for her to speak, because obviously she had something on her mind.

She scooted to the back of the chair, her feet dangling over. "Do you believe in Santa?"

"I did when I was a kid. It was the most exciting time of the year. I couldn't wait for Christmas morning to see if I'd gotten everything I'd asked Santa for."

"I'm not supposed to tell anyone, but you're an adult, right?"

He suppressed a smile. "Yeah."

She leaned toward him and whispered, "Santa's not real. Our parents put presents under the tree."

"How do you know that?" He knew the answer, but he wanted her to talk about it. It might help Lacey in her quest to get Emma to believe in Santa again.

"Brad Wilson told me and Jimmy, and it's true 'cause I asked Lacey and she doesn't lie."

"Is that why you're sad?"

Emma kicked with her feet. "My friend Bailey told me that Pepper couldn't tell Daddy my message, because dogs can't talk. That made me sad, and then I told Lacey she wasn't Daddy and she shouldn't have put up the lights."

Lacey had worked so hard on the lights. He wondered if she was over there crying. That bothered him. He didn't want her to be sad. He had to restrain himself from running to her. First, he had to talk to Emma.

"Did you apologize?"

"Yeah. Lacey said that Daddy, Pepper and Zack are in heaven, and in heaven everybody understands each other 'cause it's heaven." She raised her hands palms up to emphasize this miracle. "Lacey knows everything."

He agreed with that wholeheartedly. Lacey was wonderful.

"So why are you sad?"

"Lacey wants me to believe in Santa again, but I can't."

He scooted his chair closer. "Why not?"

"'Cause he's not real."

"You believe in heaven and you don't know that it's real."

Her eyes narrowed. "It is real. My daddy is there."

"Belief is a powerful thing. It can lift our spirits, get us through bad times and work miracles. You just have to believe sometimes. You have to trust. You believe that heaven is there because you have to know that your daddy is in a better place. I believe, too, because I have to know the same thing about Zack. I'm going solely on belief."

She looked at him, her green eyes wide. "So Santa could be real?"

He shrugged. "If your belief is strong enough, anything is possible."

Suddenly, her bottom lip trembled and he tensed. "I'm

too little to know this stuff. I just want my daddy to come back."

Gabe reached out and lifted her into his arms, trying not to let his emotions overtake him. "I want Zack to come back, too," he said, his heart tightening in pain, but he had to go on for Emma. "But there's a difference between reality and belief. And yes, you're too little to understand that. So we're not going to be sad because Lacey would be very upset with us."

Emma rested her face against his chest, and he held her as if she was the most precious thing in the world. He was beginning to believe she was. He'd thought no one could ever touch that part of him that belonged to Zack. But like her sister, Emma was working her magic on his heart.

"Oh." Emma sat up. "I forgot. Lacey said supper's ready."

"Then we'd better go. Maybe she'll dance for us."

Emma giggled. Still holding her, he stood and carried her back to her house, enjoying the feel of a child in his arms again.

Lacey was making a salad. She was cutting a tomato with more force than necessary. It was obvious she was upset.

"Go wash your hands, Emma. Supper is almost ready," she said.

Emma darted off and Gabe went into the kitchen, grabbing Lacey's arms from behind, stopping her chopping motion.

"What's wrong?"

She laid the knife on the cutting board and turned in the circle of his arms. "I'm getting everything wrong. I can't seem to do anything right concerning Emma. I keep causing her more pain."

"She told me what happened."

Her teary eyes opened wide. "She talked to you?"

"She told me what her friend Bailey said about Pepper, and that she'd hurt your feelings and she was sorry."

"You were right. I should stop all this Christmas stuff and just let her celebrate the way she wants. But I..."

He pulled her into his arms. She rested against him, and a warm glow settled around his heart. "Just take it slow. That's all you have to do. She asked me about Santa, and I think she's opening up to the idea. Just give her time. But prepare yourself for the fact that she may never believe in Santa again."

"I think I'll take down the lights tomorrow."

"Not unless she asks you to. I think I might have to explain what *slow* means."

She raised her face with a smile, and everything was right in his world in that moment. "I don't think it's in my vocabulary."

"I don't think it is, either." He turned her toward the hall. "Go take a hot bath and relax while I put supper on the table."

"I can't. I'm in the middle of making a salad."

"Go. I can finish." He gave her a gentle push and she went.

A moment later, Emma came running back. "Why is Lacey taking a bath? Did she get dirty?"

"We're giving her some time alone, so that means you have to help me."

"I can! I can!"

She was eager to help, and they had the table set and all of the food on it by the time Lacey made her appearance. That tired, sad look was gone from her face. The resilient, vibrant Lacey was back.

"Look, Lacey, we did supper, 'cause we love you."

Love. Time stood still for Gabe. Love was something he hadn't thought of because he had been unable to give it anymore. And he hadn't wanted to lead Lacey on. Or Emma. He was getting too involved, and the last thing he wanted was to hurt them.

After supper, he quickly made his exit. That might have been the coward's way out, but he needed time to think about what was happening with his feelings.

SINCE IT WAS Friday and there was no school the next day, Lacey pulled out the bag of crafts she'd bought, and she and Emma made stretchy bracelets for Emma's friends. Some had beads and some were just plain, but the important thing was that Emma was happy again.

As Lacey crawled into bed, she wondered why Gabe had left so quickly. He had been in a good mood earlier and as sweet as he could be. She smiled at that description. The grouch had turned into a sweetie. She curled up in bed and it hit her.

'Cause we love you.

She sat up. That was it. Gabe was afraid she was taking his attention for more than it was. The silly man. They were both holding on by their fingernails, and neither was ready for a serious relationship. Couldn't he see that? Silly, silly man. Tomorrow she would set him straight.

THE MORNING DIDN'T start well. Lacey burned the toast again and the smoke alarm went off. Emma covered her ears until Lacey knocked it off the wall. Gabe rushed through the back door.

"Lacey did it again, Gabe," Emma said.

"It's the toaster," she told him.

He shook his head. "You do know they sell those."

She stuck out her tongue. He ignored her and opened the kitchen window. "Seriously."

"Sit down and I'll fix breakfast."

"I just wanted to make sure everything was okay. I have work to do."

"You have time to eat eggs and toast."

He glanced at the trashcan. "It's burned."

"Oh, please. Like that's never happened before." She inserted more slices of bread.

"You have to watch it, Lacey," Emma said.

"If someone would stop distracting me, I could."

"I couldn't find my shoes."

In minutes she had toast and eggs ready for them. Gabe ate. Emma went to put on her shoes and Lacey slid onto Emma's stool.

"You know, I expect a marriage proposal for this."

His head jerked up.

"Do you really think I'm ready for a relationship? Or that you are? That's what you thought last night when Emma said y'all loved me, didn't you? You thought I wanted more from you than you're willing to give."

"More than I can give."

"I know that, Gabe. So please don't think I'm searching for a wedding dress on the internet."

He smiled and her heart lifted. "You're always surprising me."

"Sometimes I surprise myself."

Emma charged in. "I'm dressed," she announced.

Gabe slid from the stool. "I'm stacking wood to make a fire outside, and this afternoon we can do hot dogs and s'mores. My treat, since you're always cooking for me."

"Can I help you, Gabe? Please," Emma begged.

"If it's okay with your sister."

"Go, but please mind Gabe."

"I will."

Lacey expected him to go out the back door, but instead he went into the garage, got the ladder and put the smoke alarm back up.

"If you're not careful, I will be looking for that wedding dress," she whispered for his ears only.

He winked and ushered Emma out the door.

Lacey sighed and leaned against the cabinet, vowing this day would be a good day and sadness would take a break.

EMMA FOLLOWED GABE around like a shadow. He made a pile of twigs, short limbs and logs. Emma worked alongside him. He imagined she had helped Jack in the yard. He vaguely remembered a few of those times.

As he worked, he thought of Lacey's comment about him getting scared of commitment. She was right. He wasn't ready for that. It was a little uncanny that she could read him so easily. But then, they had a connection that was all tied up with grief and death. They understood pain and were struggling to find sunshine in their lives. They were becoming good friends, but part of him yearned for much more. He wasn't sure what that was at this point. All he knew was he liked being around Lacey and Emma.

Lacey came over at noon and they stopped for lunch. She had sandwiches made for them. Afterward, he said, "I'm going to the grocery store to get the things we'll need for later."

He felt energized doing something for them.

IT WAS NICE to relax and let Gabe do all the work. He had the fire blazing when she walked over and plastic-covered cushions for them to sit on. Emma was hopping around like a grasshopper, helping him. Lacey sat on a cushion, feeling like a queen.

They made hot dogs first, which tasted great after being grilled on the fire. The night air was chilly, but the fire kept them warm. Gabe had all the food on a tray and kept getting up to make sure they had everything they needed. Emma sat in front of the fire between Gabe's legs. He helped her roast a marshmallow and put it on a graham cracker with a piece of chocolate. Emma giggled and basked in Gabe's attention.

Gabe made Lacey one and fed it to her. She felt a little naughty as she ate from his fingers. The glow of the fire warmed them, but she was feeling a different kind of glow.

To still the beating of her heart, she suggested, "Let's sing songs."

"Which one?" Emma asked.

"Christmas songs, of course."

She broke into "Frosty the Snowman" followed by "Jingle Bells" and "Rudolph the Red-Nosed Reindeer." Emma joined in, and when they sang "Deck the Halls," Gabe's deep tones echoed through the night with vivid clarity and spine-tingling emotions.

Overhead, stars were showcased in a spectacular winter sky. Lacey pulled her jacket tighter around her as the temperature continued to drop. Emma's head rested on Gabe's chest. Chocolate was smeared on her face, but Lacey didn't worry about that. Emma had found a remarkable man to fill the empty place left by their father. But it was only temporary.

A chill ran through Lacey. She raised the fur collar of her jacket and scooted closer to Gabe. He looped an arm around her, and they sat listening to the snap and crackle of the fire. It was peaceful and relaxing, and Lacey allowed herself to drift into a fairy tale. She could see herself in a beautiful white gown walking down the aisle to a man with dark eyes. But she was old enough to know fairy tales didn't exist. And she'd told Gabe she wasn't interested in a relationship.

She'd lied.

Chapter Thirteen

The days passed too quickly for Lacey. Christmas was two weeks away and Emma hadn't changed her mind about Santa. The Christmas tree stood by the windows looking like a lonely soldier needing a hug. She had considered taking it down, but she would follow Gabe's advice and go slow.

He ate with them every day without complaining or making a quick exit. Having a man around was nice, especially since he was handsome and made her happy just to see him. It was too late to chide herself for letting her heart get involved. Gabe was a part of her life, but she didn't know for how much longer. She was grateful for every day and grateful he'd survived the biggest tragedy of his life. Whatever happened next would be up to them.

She still had to make arrangements to visit her mom before Christmas. Time seemed to be running out and she had a lot to do before the big day arrived. The number one goal today was to put the bicycle together. After dropping Emma at school, she hurried over to Gabe's. He sat on the floor in an empty bedroom with parts of the bike laid out.

She stared at all the bolts, screws and pieces. "When they say you have to put it together, they're not kidding."

Gabe looked up from a page of instructions. "It's really not that hard."

"I'll take your word for it." She held up the bag in her hand. "I brought paper, ribbon and tape to wrap Emma's other gifts."

She sat down and went to work. But she kept looking up to watch him, and the way his hands and arms worked with confidence and ease. His hair was really getting long. Today he had it combed back, and it hung past the collar of his T-shirt.

"Have you always worn your hair long?"

He didn't even look up as he attached the front wheel. "No. I got a haircut about two months after I moved here from the only barber shop in town. It's run by two old cowboys and they asked a lot of questions. They were just being friendly, but I wasn't in a friendly mood, so I never went back."

"It gives you a roguish-outlaw look."

He sat back on his heels, his eyes gleaming. "You like roguish outlaws?"

"If they have dark eyes."

He pointed a wrench at her. "You're distracting me."

"Me? I'm just wrapping presents."

"Mmm." He went back to the bicycle with total concentration, or at least it appeared that way.

She finished the gifts and stacked them in a corner. When she turned around, Gabe stood there with the bicycle completed.

"Oh, it's beautiful. I have to go to the house to get ribbon to put around the basket. It has to have a red bow. I'll be right back."

In a matter of minutes she had returned. She threaded a ribbon around the white basket and finished it with a big bow.

"Do you put a bow on everything?"

She straightened with a piece of ribbon in her hand. "Yes." And before he could stop her, she caught his hair and looped the ribbon around and tied it.

"Take it out," he said in a warning voice, moving closer to her.

"No. I like it." She took a step backward.

"Take it out."

"No." She stood her ground for a split second before he grabbed her. He held her hands up to his face. Their eyes met and everything faded away except the feelings between them. His head dipped and his lips captured hers in a time-standing-still type of kiss. The laughter and playfulness turned into serious emotional need. She wrapped her arms around his neck and pressed her body into his, loving the feel of his hard angles against her softer ones.

The kiss went on and on until they finally sank to the floor. His hand slipped under her blouse and touched her breast. An ache shot through her—a familiar ache she welcomed. She ran her fingers through his hair, loving the thick texture and the scent of manly shampoo.

Just when she thought the world would spin away, her cell phone rang. It took a moment for her to realize what the sound was. Gabe pulled away, back in total control.

She crawled on her hands and knees to her purse and found her phone. She couldn't let it keep buzzing. It could be about Emma. It wasn't. When Lacey saw it was her mother, she wasn't going to answer, but one look at Gabe's face and she knew the moment had passed.

"Hi, Mom."

"You haven't called about Christmas."

Christmas was the last thing she wanted to talk about

right now. "I was thinking next week one day. When can you be free?"

"Christmas Day."

Lacey wanted to pound the phone on the floor, but instead she replied, "You know that's out of the question unless you plan to come to Horseshoe."

"I guess I'm pushed aside for any old day."

Gabe put tools back into his toolbox, and Lacey was very aware of the frown on his face. Her mother's words went right over her head. "How about next Wednesday?"

"You know it's hard for me to get off during the holidays. We're so busy."

"Whatever, Mom. I've told you what I can do. I don't know what else to say except that I love you and I'd love to spend some time with you."

A heavy pause followed. "Wednesday will be fine. You can pick me up at work and we'll go to a nice restaurant."

"That sounds good. I'll see you then."

Lacey clicked off, stunned that had been so easy. Three little words had worked magic. She glanced up to see Gabe staring at her. She wondered if they would work on him. But she would never put him in that position.

"Your mom, huh?" He closed the toolbox with a snap.

"Yeah, she's finally agreed on a day for us to visit."

"I'm glad you're trying to work things out."

She disliked the stilted conversation. "Gabe, could we talk?"

"I thought we were talking." He wrapped his arms around his knees and stared at her.

"I mean about what just happened between us."

"Lacey…"

"I'm attracted to you. I think you know that, and I don't want to lie about it or pretend I'm not."

The silence stretched before he finally said, "I'm attracted to you, too. I like touching you, holding you and kissing you. And I shouldn't. I still have a long way to go for full recovery, and I don't want to hurt you."

She crawled on the hardwood floor to him and sat beside him. "You really do need furniture. Do you know that?"

A smile touched his lips. "You have a knack for lightening a mood."

"Because there shouldn't be a mood. We're both adults. What happens between us is our business, and I think we're mature enough to handle it."

He stretched out his legs and leaned back on his hands. "I can't get serious about anyone right now. I have a past I'll have to face someday. I don't want you caught in the middle."

She tickled his nose with a piece of ribbon. "You worry too much. Now, I have to go. It's my day to help out at school and I have to change. Do you mind if I leave the bicycle and gifts here until Christmas Eve?"

"No problem. But I'd better put them in the closet in case the kiddo comes in here."

After everything was stored in the closet, Lacey said, "I'll see you later."

She didn't try to kiss him or touch him because she knew he was struggling with his feelings. She was, too, but somehow she knew what she wanted. Only time would tell if it was real or just the result of being thrown together as next-door neighbors at a time when they'd each needed someone.

THE NEXT FEW days were hectic. The kids in Emma's class were rehearsing for the Christmas program. The girls were told to wear red and the boys were to wear black pants and white shirts. Emma wanted a new dress for the occasion, so they decided to go to the mall on Saturday.

Lacey only saw Gabe at mealtime. He was building a storage shed in his backyard. He seemed to have a need to stay busy. Lacey understood that, but she felt he was putting distance between them. That made her sad, but she was learning the hard way to go slow.

On Wednesday, when she drove to the school to drop off Emma, Mrs. Fillmore was waiting outside. Lacey had wanted to get away quickly so she could leave for Austin to see her mother. Emma had been exceptionally good the past week, so Lacey couldn't imagine what the teacher wanted.

Lacey kissed Emma, who ran off to meet Jimmy.

"Hello, Lacey."

"Good morning, Mrs. Fillmore."

"I know you do a lot for Emma's class, but I'd like to ask one more favor. Most of the mothers work, and I'm not getting any assistance for the Christmas program. I need someone to help me get the children on the stage where they need to be. It just takes a little patience."

"I'll be happy to help. It's next Friday, right?"

"Yes, and thank you. I'm so happy Emma is adjusting after her father's death."

"Me, too," Lacey admitted.

Mrs. Fillmore turned toward the school. "I'll let you know details next week. Have a nice day."

Lacey drove home and dressed for the day in a print skirt, silk blouse and leather boots. Her mother would expect more than jeans. She hadn't told Emma where she was going because Emma would have wanted to go, too, and explaining her mother's feelings would be difficult. She had Gabe's number on her phone, so if she was running late or had problems, she could call him to pick up Emma.

As she brushed her hair, she thought she'd better let Gabe know her plans. She slipped on the cashmere jacket her mother had given her last year for Christmas and went next door.

GABE WAS BUSY laying forms so the concrete company could pour the foundation for the shed. He looked up and saw a woman standing near his deck. Who was she? And what did she want? He got to his feet and walked toward her. The closer he got he realized it was Lacey, all dressed up and looking as beautiful as he'd ever seen her.

He wiped his hands on his jeans. "I didn't recognize you at first."

She lifted an eyebrow. "Is that good or bad?"

"I'm not sure." He was honest. "I feel as if I don't know you." He looked her up and down. "You're very different from the woman in jeans who makes me smile."

She leaned over and whispered, "I can still make you smile." A whiff of a delicate fragrance reached him, and he wanted to reach out and take her in his arms. He had the urge to get to know this Lacey. And he shouldn't. He was so tired of resisting when everything he wanted was right in front of him.

She nodded toward the forms. "Are you going to be home all day?"

"Where else would I be?"

"As you can see—" she waved a hand down her body "—I'm dressed to go visit my mother, and I wanted to make sure if I have a problem with getting back—like traffic or car problems—that someone will be there to pick up Emma. My go-to person is you. Can you help me out?"

"Just let me know and I'll be there."

She hugged him, and he wrapped his arms around her and held her for a moment. They stood there in the chilly day, and he was never more aware of how much this crazy lady had taken over his heart.

"Gotta go. I'll see you tonight. Bye."

She sashayed toward the gate, and he couldn't stop watching. Resisting wasn't an option anymore. She was pulling him in hook, line and sinker. And he wasn't panicking.

THE TRAFFIC ON I-35 was bad, but Lacey was still early for her lunch with her mother. They'd decided to meet at the restaurant. Lacey parked and went inside. Her mother had made a reservation, so Lacey was shown to a table immediately. The restaurant was very upscale with soft music playing in the background. It wasn't long before her mother arrived.

Lacey stood to hug her. Her mother was a blonde with green eyes, just like Lacey. At fifty-two, she looked more like thirty-five. Her mother had always taken care of her appearance. Today she wore a designer dress with silver earrings, a necklace and high heels.

"It's good to see you," her mother said as she took a seat. "I'm not crazy about the short hair, but it's your hair. And at your age you need to start using more makeup."

Lacey counted to three and then asked, "How's Mervin?"

"Fine. He wants me to move in with him, but I'm just not ready for that."

Her mother never shared these types of things, so Lacey was startled for a moment. Mervin was the type of man her mother should have married. He was in insurance and she assumed he was reasonably well-off.

Lacey placed a napkin in her lap. "Do you mean he wants to get married?"

Her mother glanced up, her perfectly made-up face revealing a wrinkle or two. "Of course, I would never move in with a man without marriage. I jumped into marriage too fast the second time, and I am not doing it again."

"Do you love him?"

The waiter came with menus and they ordered drinks.

"Love is for young folks," her mother said as soon as the waiter was out of earshot. "I just don't want to be alone for the rest of my life."

Guilt slashed across Lacey's conscience. Her mother had always lived her life her way, but Lacey still felt guilty for not spending more time with her.

Joyce opened her menu. "The scallops are really delicious here, and I know how you love them."

Her mother changed the subject quickly, and Lacey let it drop because she didn't know what else to say. They had a pleasant meal and chatted like strangers, not like a mother and daughter who had their ups and downs.

Lacey decided to talk about the holidays. "I wish you would come for Christmas. I want you to. Does that mean anything?"

Joyce laid her napkin on the table very carefully. "I just can't be around that child."

Lacey bit her tongue and prayed for patience. Going on her gut instinct that her mother wasn't as coldhearted as she seemed, she reached into her purse and pulled out a small photo album she kept of Emma. She opened it and laid it on the table near her mother's napkin.

"Look at Emma. She has blond hair and green eyes and looks like me." Joyce picked up her napkin and wiped her mouth, ignoring the photo. "Look, Mom. She's just a little girl. She doesn't know about divorce or resentment or regrets. She's only knows she's lost her daddy and it's still hard for her to accept. That's why she clings to me. I'm the only person there for her. Look at her, Mom."

Her mother finally glanced at the photo album. Lacey flipped it to the next picture and the next.

"She has blond hair and green eyes just like us," Joyce commented. "How is that possible?"

"Mona's eyes were green, but Emma's are lighter like mine and yours. I don't know how it's possible. I just know that it is."

"Her hair and everything about her reminds me of you when you were that age."

"Everyone who meets us comments on how alike we look."

"You were always your father's daughter."

Lacey wasn't sure how to respond to that, so she didn't, hoping it wasn't going to lead to another argument.

"Sometimes I felt left out. Your father took you to ball games and fairs and carnivals and fishing. Not once did he ask me to go."

Lacey was dumbstruck. "Because you didn't want to," Lacey reminded her.

Joyce waved a hand. "That's beside the point. It would have been nice to have been included sometimes."

"I'm sorry if we shut you out."

"And I'm sorry about a lot of things. It's hard to explain my feelings about Emma. I know they're wrong," Joyce said, leaning back in her chair. "Your father always wanted another child and I kept putting it off. I started having female problems and had to have a hysterectomy. It was too late then."

"I never knew you wanted another child."

Her mother glanced in the direction of a waiter who was clearing a table. "Jack and I argued about it all the time. I regret not listening to him more. I regret so many things, and when I see his child with another woman, I'm filled with such anger, and it's all directed at me. I screwed up our lives and I have only myself to blame."

Lacey's breath caught at her mother's obvious pain. So many years and she was learning things about her mother that she'd never known. "But Emma's not to blame. She has no grandmothers, only an aunt who doesn't know her. I'm all she has, Mom. She could use you in her life."

"Please don't ask that of me."

Lacey reached across the table and took her mother's hand. Joyce gripped it tightly. "Emma and I need you. Think about that."

They walked to their vehicles in silence. Lacey gave her mother a gift and she accepted one from her. "I'm not going to open this. I'll keep it until Christmas, hoping you'll change your mind."

They hugged and Lacey said, "I love you, Mom." She got in her car and drove away. In her rearview mirror she could see her mother still standing in the parking lot, looking lonely and alone.

Why did life have to be so hard?

Lunch had run long, and Lacey was in a hurry to get back to Horseshoe. She didn't want to be late to pick up Emma, but there was a wreck on I-35 and the traffic was backed up for miles.

She hit the steering wheel with the palm of her hand. "Damn it!"

Thirty minutes later the traffic still hadn't moved, and she knew she wasn't going to make it. She had Mrs. Fillmore's private number, so she called and told her the situation. Thank God the teacher had a heart of gold. She let Emma talk to Lacey on the phone.

"Sweetie, I'm caught in traffic and Gabe will pick you up. Okay?"

"Where are you?"

"On a highway and I can't get to school on time because someone had a wreck in front of me."

"Are you gonna come get me?"

Lacey's heart sank and she repeated, "Sweetie, Gabe will be there. I'll come as soon as the traffic clears."

"'Kay."

Clicking off, she immediately called Gabe. She tapped her fingers on the steering wheel, hoping Emma wasn't going to be upset. After another thirty minutes, the traffic began to move, and she zoomed toward Horseshoe.

It was 3:30 p.m. when she pulled into her driveway. She expected Emma to be in the front yard bawling her eyes out. She wasn't, but that didn't mean she was okay. Lacey jumped out of the car, yanked open the front door, ran through the house, out the back door and through the gate.

She stopped suddenly. Gabe and Emma were working on the concrete forms. Emma knelt in the dirt with a hammer and was beating on something. Gabe was beside her, talking and giving instructions. Emma chatted away, comfortable with Gabe and unafraid. She was okay. Lacey was, too. She took a long breath and relaxed.

Everything was perfect. Just perfect.

Chapter Fourteen

Gabe looked up, saw Lacey and whispered to Emma. Her sister jumped up and ran toward her, screeching, "Lacey! Lacey! Lacey! You're home."

Lacey caught her and lifted her into her arms, kissing her cold cheeks. "Are you okay?"

"Yeah. Gabe picked me up and we're busy working."

"I see." No tears. No fears in her beautiful green eyes. She was adjusting, and that was the best Christmas gift Lacey could receive.

Emma wiggled to get down. "I have to help Gabe."

Gabe had ambled over by then and she smiled into his dark, warm eyes. "Thank you."

"No problem."

"We got ice cream, Lacey."

"You did? That was a treat."

"Yeah. Now we have to get back to work."

Lacey hated to burst her bubble. "Sweetie, it's homework time, and I have to get supper started. You can help Gabe tomorrow."

Emma scrunched up her face. "Aw, Lacey."

Gabe squatted in front of Emma. "Tell you what, kiddo. I'm going to get cleaned up. While you're doing homework, I'll go to the diner and get supper for us. Lacey's had a rough day."

He glanced at her and as he said the last words, she thought if this wasn't love, she didn't know what was. The revelation shook her. She'd considered herself in love with Darin, but the feelings she had for Gabe were different. It was as if he held her heart in his hand and he had to squeeze it for her to breathe. Without him... She stopped herself. These feelings were too new, too soon, and she had to stop weaving dreams that weren't meant to be. She could breathe perfectly well on her own, thank you very much.

She vowed not to overthink their relationship. For now, she would enjoy his company and be thankful that he was growing stronger and stronger emotionally.

The days that followed were easygoing. Gabe continued to work on the storage shed, and she was busy helping Mrs. Fillmore with the school program. Since she wasn't home much during the day, they had very little time alone with Emma there. But it gave Lacey a chance to figure out exactly what she was feeling. She wasn't sure love was supposed to happen that quickly. But then she was a sucker for love at first...grouch.

ON SATURDAY, LACEY and Emma went to the mall in Temple to buy a dress for the program. It was a big mistake. The mall was crowded and it was hard to shop, but they finally found a dress that Emma liked and so did Lacey. It was red with a black-and-red polka-dot ribbon around the waist.

Emma wanted to get something for her teacher, so they searched for that, all the while fighting the crowds. The chatter and noise was loud and festive, and the piped-in Christmas music filled their ears. As they walked toward the entrance, they passed Santa's Wonderland, where a long line stretched into the crowd.

Lacey didn't say anything to Emma and they kept walking. It took everything in Lacey not to point out Santa. But she would not force Emma. That was more important.

Suddenly, Emma stopped and looked back. "I want to talk to Santa."

This was more than Lacey had hoped for. "Um… okay." She had no idea what Emma wanted to say, but Lacey was going to give her the opportunity. Maybe, just maybe, a miracle might happen.

They stood in line for fifteen minutes before they reached Santa.

"Hi, little girl." Santa patted his knee. "Hop right up and tell Santa what you want for Christmas."

Emma crawled onto his knee and stared him straight in the eye. "You're not real."

Lacey gasped and hoped the kid behind her didn't hear. She'd had no idea her sister was going to be this blunt.

Santa was taken aback, but only for a moment. "You don't say. You're awfully young to think that way."

"But it's true."

"Now, I know I'm not the real Santa. He's at the North Pole, awfully busy getting ready to deliver a lot of gifts to children all over the world. I'm just one of his helpers, taking children's wishes back to him."

The expression of stubbornness on Emma's face changed to one of confusion. She wasn't quite sure anymore. Lacey knew her that well. Yes! She wanted to raise her fist in the air, but she waited to hear Emma's next words.

"'Kay. I'll tell you what I want for Christmas, and if it comes true, I'll know Santa is real." Then she did something that made Lacey want to scream. She whispered into the man's ear. Lacey couldn't hear a word. She stepped closer, but the noise of the crowd prevented her from hearing.

"Santa can do some things, but others he can't. Just never stop believing," the man said, and Emma slipped off his lap.

Lacey took Emma's hand and they walked out of the mall. One way or another she was going to get Emma to tell her what she had asked Santa for.

As Lacey buckled her seat belt, she glanced at Emma. "Santa was nice."

"He's just a helper."

Lacey started the car and backed out of the parking spot, trying to be patient. "But you believe what he said to you?".

"I told him what I wanted for Christmas, and if I get it, then I'll know."

One. Two. Three. Be patient.

"What did you ask for, sweetie?"

"I can't tell you, because then I won't know if Santa is real."

Evidently a six-year-old was smarter than Lacey. Emma refused to say what she wanted for Christmas no matter how many times Lacey tried to turn the conversation in that direction. It wouldn't come true if she told Lacey, she kept saying. Lacey would give her time, but she had to find out. Above all else, she wanted Emma to believe.

GABE SPENT THE morning in Horseshoe. He stopped at a resale shop and bought a patio table and chairs for the deck. He'd seen the set as he'd passed by and had decided that he needed it. At the hardware store he purchased a barbecue pit. He was making hamburgers for

Lacey and Emma that night. From there, he went to the grocery store.

He had just finished setting things up when Lacey walked over. From her dazed expression, he knew her mind was somewhere else. She sank into one of the cushioned wrought iron chairs as if it had always been there.

He leaned against the table. "What's wrong?"

"Emma talked to Santa at the mall."

"Well, that's good. It's what you want, isn't it?" He wasn't sure because her expression didn't change.

"She told him what she wanted by whispering it to him, and now I don't know what it is. I'm trying to figure out a way to get it out of her. Nothing's working. She's adamant that if she gets what she asked for, then she'll know that Santa is real." Lacey's eyes narrowed in thought. "Think I'll go back to the mall and try to talk to the Santa and see if he'll tell me. I'll make him tell me."

"S-l-o-w." Gabe spelled out the word patiently and her head jerked up. "You're getting obsessed with this, and you need to take a deep breath, stop and think. Emma has taken a step forward, so you have to continue to let this happen naturally."

She ran both hands through her hair and fluffed it like he'd seen her do so many times when she was worried. "But if she doesn't get what she asked for, then she'll never believe and I'll…"

"You'll love her and you'll be there for her like you always are. So, please, calm down and just take it slow."

"Why are you always—" She touched the cushion beneath her. "What am I sitting on?"

"A chair cushion."

She jumped up and looked at the patio set. "You bought some furniture." Her eyes went to the barbecue pit. "And a barbecue pit. You're settling in and nesting."

Unable to resist, he pulled her into his arms. "Men don't nest."

"Mmm." She splayed her hands across his chest, and he felt their warmth all the way to his heart. She had that effect on him. "Men hunt. Isn't that a quote from Jerry Seinfeld? So what did you hunt us up for supper?"

"Hamburger meat. And it was hell beating little old ladies to it in the grocery store."

She laughed, a bubbly sound that relaxed every muscle in his body, and at the same time tightened them in a well remembered way.

"Where's Emma?"

"Inside. Jimmy was waiting in our driveway, and they're playing with Legos. I better go check on them. I just had to vent to someone, and you're my go-to guy."

"Happy to be the go-to guy. Come over later and we'll do the hamburgers."

She went down the deck steps and he called, "And stop obsessing."

She stuck out her tongue and made her way to the gate. It seemed like forever since he'd nailed the gate shut. He'd been in that deep, dark hole. Unreachable. Safe. And dying a little each day. She'd had the nerve to bring him back, and a part of him would always be grateful for that. Even though his other life waited, he couldn't see beyond this time here in Horseshoe with Lacey and Emma. If he was living in a fool's paradise, it was the best place on earth.

LACEY SPENT THE entire weekend trying to coax Emma into telling her what she wanted for Christmas. After a couple of dark looks from Gabe, she gave up. He was right, as always. It would work out the way it was meant to be, and she had to accept that.

After she left Emma at school on Monday, she put on her sweats and grabbed her iPod. Gabe had started running every morning and she planned to join him. She really needed the exercise.

Gabe walked out of his house and she met him in the front yard. He gave her a quick glance in the sweats. "What are you doing?"

She jogged in place. "I'm running with you this morning."

"I go fast and I don't stop for anything."

"I go slow and stop for everything. My attention span is not that great."

He lifted an eyebrow. "Mmm."

"I'll hang with you until I drop."

He took off down the driveway and into the street. She followed and tried to keep up with him, but she soon found his long strides too much. Somewhere around the two-mile mark she collapsed on a curb, breathing heavily.

"You okay?" he shouted back.

She waved a hand. "I'm fine."

Her heart ping-ponged inside her chest with painful thuds, reminding her she was in dismal shape. She really needed to work out every day. And she would, just as soon as she could feel her legs again.

Two cars stopped, their drivers asking Lacey if she was okay. She muttered something and they drove on. Mrs. Hornsby, on whose curb Lacey was sitting, came out and asked if she'd like a cup of coffee. The last thing she needed was coffee, but she thanked her, and the elderly lady left Lacey to her misery.

It was about 8:30 a.m. and it was nice sitting there in the cool morning. Or it would be when she could breathe normally. The winter grass was brown and brittle, and the trees had lost their leaves and stood out like stick figures against the cold. A squirrel darted across the street and up one of the trees. Several green cedars stood out in prominence as if waiting to be decorated. That reminded her of the poor Douglas fir in her living room. It probably would never be adorned with the bright colors of Christmas. She wouldn't force Emma, but it was taking a toll on Lacey's Christmas spirit.

She was about to get up when she saw Gabe jogging toward her. He wasn't even breathing hard. He squatted in front of her with his back to her.

"Hop on."

"Gabe…"

"Come on. I need coffee."

She did as he'd asked, feeling a little foolish and very young. He fitted his arms under her knees and took off toward their houses.

She wrapped her arms around his neck. "I really can walk, you know."

"You're too slow."

"You've wanted me to go slow."

"Different situation. And stop talking. It uses up too much oxygen."

She rested her face in the crook his neck and drew in the manly scent of soap and sweat. It revived her senses.

"I have Oreos and coffee waiting."

He didn't answer, just jogged up her sidewalk through the front door and dropped onto her sofa. He fell one way and she went the other. He was exhausted and she was laughing. She couldn't help herself. Then they both were laughing like teenagers.

"Well, we've given the neighbors something to talk about."

"Yeah." He rested his head back against the sofa. "Things were getting too boring."

She rose on her knees beside him. "I'll have you know I'm never boring."

He turned to look at her with a half grin. "Now, that's the gospel truth."

She poked him in the ribs, and he pulled her onto his lap, his lips finding hers with heat-seeking accuracy. She curled her arms around his neck. Her fingers tangled in his hair, and she reveled in the fire building between them. His lips were cold and hot at the same time and she felt that heat in the regions of her body that really needed it. He groaned and she opened her mouth. The kiss deepened to the point they both needed—somewhere between fantasy and reality. His lips trailed to her cheek and then to her neck. Her skin ached from his touch, and it ignited her senses into full-blown arousal. When she straddled him, not even thinking of consequences, and pressed her body against his, he pulled his mouth away.

"S-l-o-w." Each letter came out ragged, but she knew he meant it. They were going too fast. "You said something about Oreos and coffee."

She kissed the tip of his nose. "I had something else in mind."

"I know. I did, too, but..."

She slid from his lap. "I really hate that word—*but.*" She walked into the kitchen and poured coffee for both of them and then found the cookies. He took the cups to the table and she followed, feeling as if she'd already had too much caffeine. Her nerves were jiggy and she was hyped up. It was all about sex, which she hadn't really thought about in a long time. And that was good.

After sitting at the table, she opened the cookies and

handed him two. She was about to add cream and sugar to her cup when she noticed the dark liquid. It reminded her of his incredible eyes. She didn't need the coffee. All she had to do was look into his gaze and she'd receive the same thrill, the same lift and the same warm feeling.

Even so, she took a sip and looked at him over the rim. "Are you freaked out yet?"

"A little," he admitted to her surprise. "I've never felt about anyone the way I feel about you. I know we're both adults, but I come with a lot of baggage, and I don't want to drag you down."

She reached out and touched his arm. "Let me worry about that. I'm a big girl. I've been on a date before and in a serious relationship, so I know about pain and disillusionment."

He dipped an Oreo into his coffee. "But…"

She groaned. "No buts."

"The concrete people are coming today, so I better get moving." He drained his cup and stood.

"Are you running scared?"

"You betcha. You scare the hell out of me and make me feel things I haven't felt in years. So yeah, it makes me want to run."

"But not too far."

He winked and walked out the door. She finished her coffee and three Oreos. Then she got up and went to take a cold shower.

GABE HURRIED INSIDE his house, took a shower and changed clothes. A rumble of thunder echoed, and he walked to the window to look outside. The clouds had darkened, and rain softly splattered the ground. His cell phone buzzed, and he reached for it on the bed. It was the concrete company to notify him they wouldn't be coming because of the rain.

He stayed at the window and continued to watch. The rain would screw up his forms. He'd have to redo them tomorrow or whenever it stopped raining. The dirt around Pepper's grave was sinking in, and he'd have to order more dirt to fill it in.

Drawing a long sigh, he went into the kitchen and made a pot of coffee. He would just as soon have it with Lacey, but being around her was getting harder and harder. Most of the time he was frustrated, because the feelings between them were getting hotter and hotter. Soon he'd have to make up his mind about what he wanted to do: love her or admit they had no future.

He turned and saw the photos of Zack on the wall. Most of the time he would stop and look at them and remember the day each photo was taken and remember all the love and happiness that had filled his heart. But he couldn't live in the past. He already knew that.

He marched to his bedroom and pulled his briefcase out of the closet. It was empty because he'd left all of his work on his desk the day he'd left his law firm. He took it into the kitchen and laid it on the table. One by one he took down the photos. He didn't study them or remember. It was just as Lacey had said. All those memories were in his heart and they always would be. When the briefcase was full, he carried it back to his room and stored it in the closet. Tomorrow he'd work on the ones in the living room. First, he'd have to find something to put them in.

Ironically, as the rain continued to tap against the windows he didn't feel sad. He felt a release, a freedom— a freedom to move forward with his life without guilt. Without regrets. Without pain.

But he would take it slow, just as he'd told Lacey to do so many times. In the days ahead he would know what his future held.

Chapter Fifteen

On Wednesday, Lacey dashed over to Gabe's for a minute. The night before, he'd worked late on the shed after they had poured the concrete to make sure no stray dogs or cats or birds could mess up his work. Emma had gone over and written her name in the wet cement with a stick. But Lacey had had no time alone with him.

Gabe wasn't outside, which was a surprise. She knocked on the door and he opened it immediately with a cup of coffee in his hand.

"Morning," he said. "Would you like a cup?" She didn't need coffee. All she had to do was look at him and the warm fuzzies started.

"No, thanks. I'm on my way back to the school with cupcakes and stuff for the classroom party." She walked in and he closed the door. "It's the last week of school before the holidays and Mrs. Fillmore has roped me into doing all kinds of things. I just wanted to tell you that we won't be home this evening. We have the last rehearsal for the program on Friday. I'm thinking of dressing as an elf in green Lycra."

"Now, I'd go to see that."

She moved closer to him. "Would you?"

"You bet." The line of his lower lip curved into a smile

and she had the urge to kiss it and to never stop. Instead, she moved into his arms.

He placed his cup on the counter and enveloped her in his warm embrace, and she floated away on that feeling.

"You feel so good," she whispered.

He took a step back. "We'd better stop because you have to go to school. Remember?"

"Oh, yeah. Mrs. Fillmore."

He tucked her hair behind her ear and then touched the frown on her face. "What's bothering you?"

She heaved a sigh. "Emma's friend Bailey is having a birthday/slumber party on Friday night and she's invited Emma. That's a problem. Since Dad passed away, Emma hasn't been away from me except to go to school. She's all excited about it, but I'm just not sure. I feel she's too little to stay away at night."

"Then say no."

"But… I can't believe I'm saying *but*."

He cupped her face in his hands and she lost all train of thought. "Don't think it to death. Things might change by Friday, but if she wants to go I would support her and encourage her. She's improved so much."

She rested her face against his chest and stared at a blank wall. Then she pulled back quickly. "The photos are gone."

"I took them down the other day. It was time. I still have the ones in the living room, but I intend to take them down, too."

She threw her arms around his neck and hugged him. "I'm so proud of you."

He held her against him, and their emotions began to swirl into another direction. Lacey pulled away. "I really have to go. I don't want to, but…" She laughed.

He laughed with her. It was an effort to leave him.

The grouchy man had disappeared and in his place stood a man who was becoming more and more a part of her life. She didn't freak out. And neither did he. That was the good part. Christmas was going to be wonderful.

LACEY MADE IT through the week. The children's program went off with a few glitches, but they were six-year-olds so everyone laughed and understood. All the kids, including Emma, were eager to be out of school for the holiday. She chatted on and on about Bailey's party. Lacey had decided to let her go. She had talked to Bailey's mother and the woman understood the situation and had said she would call if Emma became distressed.

But Emma appeared fine as she marched to the front door with her little suitcase in hand. Bailey and her mother stood there. Emma waved and Lacey had to force herself to drive away. What if Emma needed her?

Go slow. Don't obsess. She repeated the words several times until she felt better.

She kept her cell phone in her pocket as she fixed dinner for her and Gabe. It was going to be special. She'd gotten the menu of salmon, fresh asparagus and roasted potatoes from the internet.

Gabe was outside framing the shed. It wasn't long before he knocked at her back door and came in. When she saw him, the spoon in her hand clattered to the tiled floor. She hardly recognized him. He'd cut his hair into a neat, short style. She could only stare. He was clean shaven and his hair was damp from a shower. He'd made an effort for tonight, and her pulse soared at the thought. His dark good looks and light blue shirt held her attention. It was the first time she'd seen him in any color other than black.

She smiled at him. "Love the look."

He touched his head. "I braved the barbershop again and it wasn't so bad. I found this shirt in my closet." He slid onto a bar stool. "How did it go with Emma?"

"So far so good." Lacey picked up the spoon from the floor and put it in the sink. "I'm the only one feeling a little stressed. I just don't want her to panic when she realizes I'm not there."

"If that happens, someone will call you."

She placed some cheese and grapes in front of him. "I've figured that out. So I'm trying to relax." She reached for the bottle of wine on the counter and handed it to him. "And looking forward to relaxing a little more."

"I see."

They drank wine, talked, ate and enjoyed just being together. They cleaned the kitchen and then took their wine to the living room. A college-bowl game was on television and Gabe wanted to watch.

"You like football?" she asked.

"Doesn't every guy?"

She curled into his side, trying to show interest in the game, but with his body so close that was impossible. She picked up his hand and linked her fingers with his bigger ones.

"Can I ask you a question?"

"Sure." He looked at her then.

"How do you see this night ending?"

"I'm hoping the Tigers will win," he said, deadpan.

"Um…I'm not talking about the game. I…" He pushed her down on the sofa and her voice trailed off.

"Your lips need a little red."

She giggled like a silly schoolgirl.

His lips met hers and she wrapped her arms around his neck, reveling in his touch and the feel of him. His hand slid beneath her sweater to her breast, creating a vibrating need within her.

"Too many clothes," he breathed. With one swift movement he stood and swept her into his arms.

As he headed for the hallway, she said, "First door on the left."

They didn't bother with the light. She slid from his arms, their bodies never losing contact. Clothes became an encumbrance and soon they were scattered on the floor as they frantically helped each other. His boots took more time to shed than either of them wanted. A bubble of laughter erupted as they fell onto the bed, arms and legs entwined. This was the way it should be. Warm skin. Male skin. So rough. So enticing. So what she needed.

"Lacey…" His ragged voice seemed to come from far away, but she heard the question in it.

"Don't think," she whispered. "Please."

His lips left the well of her mouth and trailed to her breast, and she wanted to scream from the sheer bliss of his breath on her sensitive nipple. His hands touched every part of her while hers were equally at work on him. Her fingers found the taut muscles of his arms, shoulders, rib cage and then moved lower. She'd never touched anything as heavenly as his aroused body.

It could have been seconds, minutes or an hour before his body finally joined with hers. All she knew was it was the most exquisite pleasure she'd ever experienced. She welcomed him with a fever that brought them both to the brink of total ecstasy.

Somewhere between need and the ecstasy, she moaned, "I love you."

He stilled for a moment, but didn't say the words back. She hadn't expected them, but she had to admit it hurt a little. The sting vanished as he gathered her into his arms and rocked her gently. They lay entwined, their bodies bathed in sweat, their breathing less labored. Lacey didn't want to ever move again. She wanted this moment to last forever, with their skin touching and the world unable to intrude and ruin the moment.

A nagging chime roused her. Her cell phone! She jumped from bed and reached for it in the pocket of her jeans on the floor. It was Bailey's mother.

She quickly clicked on and glanced at the clock. It was barely 8:00 p.m. "Hello."

"Lacey, it's Denise. I hate to bother you, but I think Emma wants to come home. She's said about four times that it's dark and Lacey is probably scared."

"Can I talk to her, please?"

Emma came on the line quickly. "Hi, Lacey."

"You want to come home, sweetie?"

"Yes." No hesitation. No doubt.

"I'll be right there."

"It's dark, Lacey."

"I know. Get your suitcase. I'm on my way."

Lacey hurriedly slipped into jeans and pulled her top over her head.

Gabe sat up in bed. "Is Emma okay?"

"She just wants to come home. I'll be right back." She started for the door and then turned. "Please don't overthink what I said. We'll talk about it later."

Within seconds, she was in the car and backing out of the driveway. She so badly wanted to go back inside and be with Gabe, but Emma pulled her in another direction. Emma was more important this time.

GABE SCOOTED TO the edge of the bed and ran his hands over his face. What had he done? He'd gone with his feelings, but now it felt wrong. Lacey loved him, and that wasn't supposed to happen. He wasn't ready. He needed her, but need wasn't love. Oh, man. He'd screwed up and now he had to hurt her. That would kill him.

He found his clothes and slipped into them. In the kitchen, he poured the little bit of wine that was left down the drain, washed the wineglasses and put them away. He went out the back door and to his house. As he entered, loneliness engulfed him and a smothering feeling came over him. He took a couple of deep breaths. His chest ached and his emotions were raw.

He should've thought the situation over a little more, but he'd wanted her. At the time that had been all that had mattered. But now her emotions were involved and his were still steeped in the past. He'd come a long way, but he wasn't ready for a serious relationship. Lacey should have a man who could love her for who she really was, not a man who was still struggling to get through each day. Now he would have to step back and disappear from her life. But he didn't know how to do that. Breaking her heart would also break his. He needed her, but he didn't love her the way she deserved.

How did he tell her that?

It STARTED TO drizzle as Lacey parked in front of Bailey's house. The umbrella was somewhere, but she didn't take time to look for it. Emma was standing at the front door in her pj's, her suitcase in hand. Denise stood behind her.

Lacey jumped out, ran up the walk, spoke to Denise and lifted Emma into her arms. Without another word she ran to the car as the rain started in earnest. She put Emma in her booster seat and dashed to the driver's side.

Emma didn't say anything as Lacey drove the three blocks to their house. As she parked in the garage, she noticed that Emma was sound asleep. She lifted her out of the car and carried her into the house. Emma awoke as Lacey tucked her into bed.

"It's raining," Emma murmured.

"Yes, it is, but you're safe at home."

"I wasn't scared," Emma stated.

Lacey kissed her sister's forehead. "I know, sweetie. Go to sleep."

Thunder rumbled outside and Emma jumped. "Sleep with me for a while, Lacey."

She was torn between going to her room to see if Gabe was still there or assuaging her sister's fears. The sensible part of her brain told her Gabe would have left long ago. "I have to get out of these wet clothes. I'll be right back."

"Lacey?"

Pulling a big T-shirt over her head, Lacey called back, "I'm coming."

She climbed in with Emma and cuddled with her. In seconds, Emma was asleep again.

When Emma became restless, Lacey slipped from the bed and made her way to her room. She grabbed the pillow Gabe's head had been on and curled up. Thunder continued to echo and lightning occasionally streaked across the sky. The tip-tap of the rain against the window lulled her to sleep.

Before she succumbed completely, she relived their night together. It had been more than she'd ever expected. She hadn't meant to say "I love you." The words had just slipped out in the heat of the moment. She had to make sure Gabe realized she didn't expect anything from him. But in her heart she knew she was lying. Her expectations might surprise him, though. Having him around was enough for her. Her responsibility to Emma would prevent her from having a life of her own for a while.

Gabe made her life a little brighter, and she hoped he understood that. The way she felt about him could cause some problems, because she knew he wasn't ready for any type of love.

Why not? The question echoed through her mind as darkness claimed her.

THE NEXT MORNING, Lacey overslept. It was after nine when she woke up with Gabe's pillow in her arms. Baby sis was sound asleep, too. Lacey had cereal and a banana ready when Emma climbed onto the stool, brushing hair from her face. She'd slept rough and her hair was everywhere.

"I don't like it when it's dark," Emma said.

"I know, sweetie. Eat your cereal."

Lacey's phone buzzed and she picked it up from the counter. It was Denise.

"I'm so sorry about last night."

Lacey walked into the living room so her sister couldn't hear. "It's okay. I had my doubts that she would stay."

"When the thunder started, all the little girls wanted to go home and Bailey was disappointed. So today we're having a big party with pedicures and manicures and princess gowns with an old-fashioned tea party. It's going to be fun, and we'd like for Emma to come back. The other girls are coming back, too."

"I'll talk to her and let you know." She hung up the phone. "Sweetie, that was Bailey's mother. They're having the party today with all kinds of fun stuff. They want to know if you want to join them."

"Do I have to stay the night?" Emma asked around a mouthful of cereal.

"No. It's just for the day."

"'Kay, but you'll come get me when it gets dark?"

"You bet. Now, we'd better hurry to get there in time for the tea party."

Emma jumped off the stool. "Oh, boy!"

Thirty minutes later Lacey once again delivered Emma to Bailey's birthday party. She waited in the car for at least ten minutes to make sure Emma was okay.

Hurrying home, she planned to take the cupcakes she had made for last night to Gabe. They had been too busy with each other to eat dessert. And they really needed to talk.

GABE SAT NURSING a cup of coffee and a foul mood. He had to talk to Lacey, but Emma was home and he wasn't sure when he'd have the opportunity for a private conversation. It was important, though, that he do it as soon as possible.

His doorbell rang and he got to his feet. Was it Lacey? She never came to his front door. At least, she hadn't recently. He opened the door in stunned disbelief. Dana, his ex-wife, stood there.

"Did you think I'd never find you?" She walked past him into the living room without an invitation. She stared at the photos on the wall. "Oh, my God, Gabe. Take the photos down. It's time to let our son rest in peace."

"What are you doing here, Dana?"

She had on a dark suit with a cream silk blouse— the kind she usually wore to work. Glancing around the room, she said, "Could we talk somewhere besides this depressing room?"

He walked into the kitchen with her a step behind him. "Would you like a cup of coffee?"

"No. This won't take long."

"How did you find me?"

"Your sister, Kate. I've called her at least three times in the past year, and she said she didn't know where you were. Then I called again last week and she finally told me."

"She didn't know for a long time where I was. I didn't want to see anyone."

"You can't keep hiding, Gabe. It's time to start living again. That's what I'm doing. I've met a man. A lawyer, actually, and we want to get married on Valentine's Day. But you left without signing the divorce papers. I really need you to do that."

"I thought I signed them."

"You didn't."

He couldn't speak. His old life had found him and he could feel the walls closing in. He fought to breathe. Fought to maintain his composure. He managed a couple of deep breaths.

"I'm glad you've found someone." He meant every word, but part of him felt a loss he couldn't describe. But then, he knew what it was. Dana was his last link to Zack. He'd thought it had been Pepper, but it was Zack's mother.

"What's wrong with you? You're very pale."

He ran a hand through his hair. "It's just seeing you and realizing once again that we've lost our son."

Her perfectly made-up face crumpled like a tissue. "Please, Gabe. Don't do this. I'm trying to live with it and move on."

He collected himself. "Okay. I'll sign the papers. Can you send them to me?"

"You have to return to Austin. We have to sell the house and go through Zack's things. We've never done that and I'm not doing it alone. I just can't."

The walls pushed in a little closer. He wanted to fight

back and not let the pain return, not let that dark hole suck him back in. The only way to do that was to face that terrible time. He knew that as well as he knew his own name. Lacey had helped him take so many steps forward. Now he had to take the final one himself.

"I'll be there in a couple days."

"Good. I've been making the payments on the house from your check, which I have deposited every month."

"The firm is still sending me checks?"

"They're expecting you to come back. Don't you understand that?"

No, he didn't. When he'd left, he'd told the senior partner that he was done and wouldn't be returning.

When he didn't respond, Dana added, "Everyone wants to help you. You just have to let them."

He drew air into a chest that was slowly collapsing. "I'm sorry I left you with all that responsibility, but I knew we had money in the account to cover it. I had no idea the firm would keep me on the payroll."

"Just come home, Gabe. We have to end our marriage. We have to end so many things."

"I'm not sure where our marriage went wrong, but it was over a long time before Zack's accident."

"It started to deteriorate when I pressured you to work for a big law firm. You resented that, even though you wouldn't admit it. Your idea was working alone in a tiny office as a private attorney. I wanted better things for our life. I wanted money to do those things, so I pushed and you withdrew. Your idea of a fun weekend was spending it on Rebel Ranch with Zack. That was a nightmare for me." She tossed her long dark hair back. "In college I thought we were compatible, but once we started living our dream we both realized we weren't. By then we had Zack and we centered our lives on him. That's why his passing hit us so hard." She studied the tip of her high-heeled shoe. "I'm sorry I blamed you for Zack's death. I was just grief stricken."

"I'm sorry I blamed you for the same reason."

She raised her eyes to his. "Then let's end this relationship amicably."

Before Gabe could respond, a knock sounded on his back door and Lacey came in with a cupcake in each hand. She looked from Gabe to Dana.

"I'm sorry. I didn't realize you had company."

Dana stepped forward. "I'm Dana, Gabe's wife."

An expression shifted across her face, as if she'd been blindsided by an eighteen-wheeler. Gabe wanted to go to her and reassure her, but his pain kept him grounded.

"Oh…um…" She moved backward out the door. "I'll just…go."

"No need," Dana said. "I was just leaving."

But Lacey wasn't listening. She disappeared down the steps, and he knew she was running to her house with tears in her eyes. His body trembled at the thought that he'd hurt the one person he cared most about in this world.

"My cell number is the same," Dana was saying. "I'll expect you in Austin before Christmas."

Gabe was aware of Dana leaving, but he had only one thought on his mind. He had to get to Lacey.

Chapter Sixteen

Lacey marched into her house, set the cupcakes on the table and then grabbed a carton of milk out of the refrigerator. She didn't bother with a glass. Sitting down, she said a curse word, peeled the paper away on one of the cupcakes and started to eat.

He was married. He was still married ran through her mind like a crazed rat on a little Ferris wheel. She'd had sex with a married man. She took a gulp from the carton and set it back on the table. The more cupcake she stuffed into her mouth, the angrier she got. How could Gabe do this to her? So much for her fantasies and dreams. Crap! She was pitiful thinking there might be a life for her and Gabe. The reality check was a downer.

Her back door opened and Gabe walked in. She kept eating. He sat on the chair next to her and she wanted to move away—far, far away from all the heartache he was about to dump on her.

"Isn't one of those for me?"

"Not anymore."

"Where's Emma?"

"She went back to her friend's house." Lacey hadn't meant to answer him, but the words slipped out.

"We need to talk."

She took a gulp of milk. "I think *wife* pretty much says it all."

"Lacey—"

"Please leave. I'm busy."

"I'll get you a glass."

"You will *not* get anything in my house. Please leave." She stuffed more cupcake into her mouth.

He picked up a napkin from the table. "You have chocolate all over your face."

"So? That's none of your concern."

"Lacey, listen to me. Can you do that without wanting to smear chocolate in my face?"

She couldn't answer because she was about to choke on the cupcake. She coughed, sputtered and grabbed the carton of milk. It took a moment, but she finally swallowed the mass of cake in her throat. She felt like a total fool.

He pushed the napkin toward her and she wiped her mouth.

"Yes, I'm still married—technically. When I left Austin a year ago, I just forgot to sign the divorce papers. Now Dana has met someone and is planning to get married, so she wants me to wrap things up and make it legal."

Lacey reached for the milk and realized she was drinking out of a plastic container. God, she was a mess. But she focused on what he was saying.

"So you're going back to Austin?" The words sounded just as bad as they'd felt inside her heart.

He took the napkin and wiped chocolate from her face. So gently. So Gabe. She wanted to cry, but refused to be that weak.

"I tried for a solid year to deal with Zack's death in every way I could, but it just got worse. I couldn't stand being around people. I couldn't stand the looks, the stares and the sympathy. One day some lawyers were laughing in the conference room and I lost it. How dare they laugh when my son was dead? The thought set me off and I said things I don't even remember, but afterward I walked out. I got in my truck, drove to the house and picked up Pepper. I started driving and ended up here. You know the rest."

She studied the poinsettia she had on a table in the corner. The red leaves heralded the beauty of the holiday season. But there was nothing beautiful about the pain in his voice.

"I just went through the motions of living, if you can call it that. I ate just enough to keep me alive. Pepper's health was what kept me going. As long as she was with me, that was all I needed. But I knew I would have to let her go and I didn't know how to do that. Until you. You were like sunshine and smiles all rolled into one. New and exciting. No matter how much I yelled at you or threatened you, you still came back, just like the blasted sun, every day. And you made me angrier than I've ever been. How dare you invade my darkness?"

"Gabe…" Her throat ached and she couldn't say another word.

"Then a miracle happened. The sunshine in you slowly sparked a light in me, and the darkness started to fade. I've loved seeing you, talking to you, being with you. I've used you as a crutch to bring myself back to life. You've saved me in more ways than one, and for that I will never forget you."

He was leaving.

A choked sob left her throat without her even knowing it. She prayed she could keep the tears inside, but she feared she was failing.

"Last night should never have happened."

She finally found her voice. "No, don't say that."

Please, don't say it meant nothing to you.

"I'll remember it always, but now it makes it that much harder to leave."

She swallowed something that tasted like fear, panic gripping her system like water filling a drowning person's lungs.

"I've been hiding from my responsibilities in Austin. I have to go back and apologize to the partners of the firm. Dana and I still haven't sold our house, and we need to do that. And we have to go through Zack's things and give them away. I'm not sure I can, but because of you I know that I'm stronger and I will try my best." He crushed the napkin in his hand. "Living next door to you has been an epiphany. I never knew people like you existed—kind, loving and selfless. In a perfect world I would stay and life would go on. We'd ignore the outside world and all the problems that could tear us apart. But that would be unfair to you."

"Wh-why?"

"Last night, when you told me you loved me, I knew I would have to disappear from your life."

"Wh-why?"

"Because I don't know what love is anymore. I need you, but I'm unable to love you the way you deserve to be loved—by a whole man who won't drag you down with sadness. Please understand that I have to go."

Her heart exploded in her chest. It shattered into a million little pieces and bled until she couldn't breathe. She didn't want to breathe. Life suddenly wasn't worth living. But there was Emma... And for her, Lacey found the strength to choke out a breath.

"When will you leave?" Her voice was low and weepy. She couldn't help it.

"I want to finish the shed first. I promised Dana I'd be there by Christmas."

She lifted her eyes to his. "You won't be here for Christmas?"

"No. Christmas doesn't mean much to me anymore. You'll be fine. Don't worry too much about Emma. She'll adjust because she has you."

But you won't be here.

Silence intruded in a way it never had before. Awkward. Painful. Then she did something to alleviate the pain of parting. It might have been wrong, but she couldn't help herself.

"Are my lips red?"

His face, etched in pain, relaxed. "No."

"They need to be. Badly."

He reached for her then and pulled her onto his lap. Her arms went around his neck and their lips met in a sweet, touching kiss that turned passionate instantly. They kissed with everything in them. They kissed as if it was their last time. Because it was. Finally, she rested her forehead against his, and this time the silence was soothing. Comforting. But only for that moment.

"I'll talk to Emma," he whispered against Lacey's face. His warm breath fanned her heated cheeks.

"You'll let me know when you're leaving?"

"I wouldn't leave without saying goodbye." He stood and gently held her elbows as she stood, too. He gazed into her eyes for a moment and then walked out, much the same way he'd done the first weeks she had known him.

She wrapped her arms around herself to still the ache in her chest, to still all the fears that gripped her and to still the tears clinging to her eyelashes. Finally, she gave up and went to her room and cried like she'd never cried before. She'd found someone special and now she'd have to learn to live without him.

Lacey wasn't sure how long she stayed in her room for the biggest pity party in the world. Afterward, she was prepared to face whatever she had to. She knew she had to let Gabe go. He had to find the peace he needed. The peace he deserved. And she had to have the strength to let him go without guilt. That would be the hardest part of all.

BESIDES HER FATHER'S illness and death, the next couple of days were the hardest Lacey had ever lived through. Gabe worked tirelessly on the shed. Even in the late hours of the night she could hear hammering, drilling and the buzz of a saw. She had invited him to eat several times, but he always refused, so she knew he was eating little and working himself until he couldn't think. She couldn't stop his pain, so she left him alone.

Emma wasn't as understanding. She was over there every day to help Gabe, as she put it. He hadn't told her yet that he was leaving. Lacey dreaded that moment. Too many people had left Emma. Lacey wasn't sure how her sister was going to take it. But she would be there to comfort her and hopefully they both would get through it.

On Tuesday afternoon, Gabe came over. Lacey was making Christmas cookies using a recipe she'd gotten from a cooking show. Emma was thoroughly enjoying decorating them with icing, sprinkles and candy pieces.

Emma was on her knees on a stool. Gabe slid onto the one next to her. He was dressed in jeans, the blue shirt and boots. He was clean shaven and his hair was combed. *He was ready to go.* Tiny pinpricks of pain shot through Lacey, but she resolved to be strong.

"Want a cookie?" Emma held out one to him.

"No, thanks, kiddo. I want to talk to you."

Emma sank back on her heels. "'Kay."

Gabe's throat worked, but no words came out, and Lacey wanted to reach across the counter and hug him so it would be easier. But she resisted with everything in her.

"I have to go back to Austin."

"Why?"

"I was very sad and down when I left, and now I have to go back and face my responsibilities. You might not understand that, but I have a house there and I need to sell it. And I have to go through Zack's things. I never did that."

Lacey held her breath for what seemed like an eternity. The emotions on Emma's face shifted and Lacey couldn't gauge what her sister was thinking. Then she did something remarkable. She held out her arms to Gabe and he lifted her onto his lap.

"Don't be sad, Gabe."

He kissed her forehead and held her. "Would you do something for me?"

Emma nodded.

"Would you take care of Pepper's grave and make sure those pesky birds don't dig around too much?"

"'Kay. I'll take care of it real good. When will you come back?"

The question that Lacey couldn't bring herself to voice Emma asked without hesitation.

"I don't know, kiddo. I have a lot of things to take care of and figure out about myself. Just know that I have to go."

Emma hugged him. "Don't be sad. Wait!" Emma jumped from his lap and ran to her room. She came back with one of the wide, stretchy woven bands. It was yellow. "Lacey and I made it for you."

Gabe slipped it onto his left wrist. "Thank you." He glanced at Lacey. His eyes, which lately had been happy and sparkly, were now dark and foreboding. All the old pain had slipped back to grip him. He walked around the counter and took her in his arms. She rested against his chest, loving this last moment with him. And hating it at the same time. The frantic pounding of his heart told her how hard this was for him, too.

"Take care of yourself. I'll remember you always." Saying that, he released her and fished a key out of his pocket. "You might need this."

She took the key and they stared at each other for endless moments. He was the first to break eye contact. "Lacey…"

"It's okay." The words came out soaked with tears but she couldn't help it. "Please find the peace you so deserve."

He inclined his head. "You'll always be my crazy lady," he whispered for her ears only. "Goodbye."

She didn't say the words back to him because she couldn't. She would never say goodbye. Ever.

He walked to her front door and she and Emma followed. Without glancing back, he strolled to his truck, which was parked at the curb, and got in. Slowly, the truck pulled away. They watched as he stopped at the street sign and then disappeared out of sight.

And out of their lives.

CHRISTMAS EVE ARRIVED cold and windy. Lacey spent the day getting ready for the holiday. She put on a brave face for Emma, but every moment she wondered what Gabe was doing and if he was okay.

Tonight when Emma went to bed, she would go over to Gabe's house, get the gifts and lock his house up for the last time. He'd never said what he planned to do with the house, and she feared one day she would come home to see a for-sale sign in the front yard. Then she'd know for sure that he would never return. But until then she'd allow herself a tiny grain of hope.

Emma was busy wrapping something in her room. Lacey had no idea what it was. She had her Christmas dinner organized. She was going to make a roast with all the trimmings for her and Emma. Once again it would just be the two of them, but she would do her best to make the day as fun as possible.

Lacey called her mom several times, but Joyce never answered. Finally, she left a Merry Christmas message.

That afternoon she and Emma got dressed to go to the big celebration on the square. The Wiznowski Bakery closed at four. Coffee, hot chocolate and free kolaches would be offered to everyone until they ran out. Then the store would be closed until after Christmas.

Everyone was in the square, eating kolaches, drinking coffee and chatting. Everyone was happy, especially when it grew dark and the huge Christmas tree in front of the courthouse was lit. Some of the kids began to sing songs, and Lacey enjoyed a moment of happiness with Peyton and Angie, but it was fleeting.

Later, Lacey and Emma put flowers on their dad's and Mona's graves, then attended the eight-o'clock mass. The church was packed. The Wiznowski family sat in the second and third rows on the left. Lacey and Emma slid into the last pew. Even though she was surrounded by people, Lacey had never felt as lonely as she did at that moment.

Erin got up and walked back to them. "Mama wants you to sit with us."

Lacey almost burst into tears, which was silly, but she was feeling a little emotional. She and Emma squeezed in with the big Wiznowski family. The service was moving and Emma sat very still beside her. Candles were passed out and lit and then the church's lights were turned off. The congregation sang "Silent Night." It was moving and touching, especially since Emma sang right along with everyone.

As they walked out into the cold night air, Angie said, "Please come for dinner tomorrow. We'll have tons of food and we'd love to have you."

"Thank you," Lacey replied. "That's very nice, but I have dinner already planned for us." She'd told Angie about Gabe leaving, so Angie knew she was feeling lonely.

"If you change your mind, just come," Angie told her.

Lacey walked away feeling good about the friends she'd made in Horseshoe. She and Emma weren't really alone, so she couldn't explain why she felt otherwise.

Back at the house they changed into their Christmas pajamas: red-and-black-plaid ones with feet and Santa Claus hats. Emma looked adorable. Lacey looked ridiculous. But it was fun.

"We have to watch Ralphie," Emma said. "Daddy and me always watched it on Christmas Eve."

"I know, sweetie, but let's have a snack first."

Emma climbed onto a bar stool. "What kind of snack?"

"A sandwich."

"Peanut butter and jelly."

"Grilled cheese," Lacey shot back.

"No, Lacey. PB&J."

"Okay, since it's Christmas."

Neither of them ate very much, and soon Emma was running into the living room to turn on the TV. Lacey sat in her dad's chair and Emma squeezed in beside her as *A Christmas Story* began.

Emma giggled every time Ralphie or Randy did something silly. Her laughter was what Lacey wanted to hear. Her sister was happy. Maybe this Christmas wouldn't be too bad after all.

Lacey was almost asleep when Emma sat up. "Lacey, our tree is not decorated. Why haven't you decorated our tree?"

Lacey blinked like a deer caught in a hunter's crosshairs. "Really? Seriously?"

"Daddy always decorated it after Thanksgiving. What's taking you so long?"

Lacey sat up. "Are you kidding me? Aren't you the kid who said you didn't believe in Santa anymore and you didn't want to decorate the tree?"

Emma shrugged. "I'm a kid. What do I know?"

Lacey grabbed her and tickled her rib cage. "I'm gonna tickle you senseless."

Emma wiggled and screamed, "No, Lacey, no!"

After a few minutes of roughhousing, Lacey got to her feet. "Let's decorate this tree. It's long overdue."

Emma had relented. That in itself was a miracle. Lacey got the decorations out of the attic. It was past midnight when they finished putting the last ornament on the tree. Lacey turned it on and the bright lights glowed, welcoming Christmas into the Carroll house. Finally.

"It's beautiful, Lacey."

She picked up her sister as if she was two years old. "Now let's go to bed and wait for Santa." Lacey didn't have to say it twice. Emma was already half-asleep on her shoulder. Lacey tucked her in and sat for a moment with her.

She gazed out the window at the cold night and wondered where Gabe was. Was he in a hotel room all alone? Was he thinking of them? Was he hurting?

Getting up, she sighed and tucked the blanket tighter around Emma. *S-l-o-w.* How she wished she could tell Gabe that Emma had decorated the tree. His advice had worked.

Lacey slipped into bed and clutched her pillow a little tighter. "Merry Christmas, Gabe. Wherever you are."

Chapter Seventeen

Lacey woke to a light touch on her cheek. She didn't freak out or scream. She knew it was Emma. Her sister had done this a lot since their father passed away. She'd wake up and sneak into Lacey's bed.

"What's up, snuggle bunny?"

"There's no Santa, Lacey."

Lacey opened one eye and stared at the clock on her nightstand. It wasn't even 5:00 a.m. "Did you look in the living room?" She'd spent over an hour putting out toys and gifts.

"I did and I saw my bicycle and lots of other stuff. I like my bicycle. I sat on it and everything."

Lacey scooted up in bed. "How long have you been up?"

"I don't know."

Lacey was trying to figure this out, but her brain was still in sleep mode. "Why are you saying there's no Santa Claus? We decorated the tree and you were happy. What has you so down this morning?"

"There's no Santa Claus, Lacey." Her sister's voice rose as if Lacey was hard of hearing.

"Okay, I hear you, but you'll have to explain because I'm still half-asleep."

"I didn't get what I asked Santa for at the mall."

Oh, good heavens. She'd forgotten about that with everything that had happened with Gabe. "What did you ask Santa for?"

"I asked for a puppy and there's not one in the living room."

Lacey wanted to smack herself on the forehead. A puppy! That was so easy. How could that have escaped her?

"I asked for two other things and I didn't get them, either. There's no Santa Claus. He's not real." Emma curled up beside her, a sad, forlorn little figure.

Lacey gathered her sister close. "What else did you ask for?"

"I...I asked for Daddy to come back one more time so I could tell him I loved him."

"Oh, sweetie." Lacey hugged Emma tight. "Santa can't grant those kinds of requests. He deals with toys. You asked him for something very personal and difficult."

"I don't care. If he was real, he could make it happen. You told me if I believed strong enough, it would happen. And I believed right here—" she jabbed a finger into her chest "—real hard and I didn't get what I asked for."

Lacey was wildly flipping the pages of the book in her head for an answer to soothe her sister's wounded heart. But she feared there was no answer for this. No answer for the dreams or wishes of a six-year-old girl.

Lacey glanced at the window. It was still dark outside, but moonlight streamed in with bright promises. Lacey was trying to figure out how to find a puppy on Christmas Day. If she called around, perhaps someone would know and maybe she could get a puppy before the day was over. And Emma would still believe. That might be wrong, but Lacey was determined to make this day as special as possible.

"I didn't get the other thing I asked for, either."

Lacey looked down at her sister. "How many things did you ask for?"

Emma held up three fingers. "I asked that Gabe would be with us forever."

Lacey was lost for a response. It was all tangled up with her own emotions of having to let Gabe go. How could this day be happy when they were so miserable?

In that moment Lacey decided she wasn't going to do this. She wasn't going to sink into a well of despair. It was Christmas and they would have Christmas.

With her thumb and forefinger she touched the corners of Emma's mouth. "Smile, snuggle bunny. We're going to have Christmas, and we're going to laugh and be happy and open our gifts and be grateful for what we have. Daddy would want us to do that."

"Yeah." Emma rose to her knees. "Let's open gifts. We don't need no Santa Claus."

"You got it." Lacey crawled from the bed. "I'll make coffee and hot chocolate and we can eat some of our delicious cookies."

"Just don't make any toast, Lacey. We don't want to burn the house down today." Emma laughed and ran into the living room.

Lacey kept forgetting to buy a new toaster. Oh, well, maybe one day she would remember. She made the coffee and hot chocolate and carried it to the coffee table in the living room.

She sat cross-legged on the sofa, sipping coffee, hoping it would wake her up. She'd only had a few hours of sleep.

"I have to get our hats." Emma dashed off again and

came back with their red-and-white Santa hats. Lacey slipped hers on, as did Emma.

Emma clapped her hands. "Now we have to open presents."

"Drink some of your hot chocolate. The marshmallows are melting."

Emma lifted the mug to her lips and drank, leaving a marshmallow ring over her upper lip, which she licked off with her tongue.

"What gift do you want to open first?" Lacey asked.

"You have to open yours first. I'll go get it." Once again, Emma charged off and came back with a wad of wrapping paper around something. Every inch of the red and green paper had tape on it. "I wrapped it myself."

"I see."

"You're gonna love it. Open it! Open it!" Emma's eyes flashed like a Fourth of July sparkler.

"You're excited."

"Yeah."

"Remember, I told you that sometimes giving is better than receiving. You're excited and can't wait for me to see your gift." She reached over and touched Emma's chest. "That feeling in there is what Christmas is all about."

"It feels like jumping beans are in there."

Lacey smiled, placing her cup on the coffee table. "Well, then, I better open this before you explode."

She could hardly tear the paper away for Emma's little face being in the way and the tape that constantly stuck to her fingers. Emma had probably used a whole roll of tape. As she peeled the last piece of paper away, she saw a piece of Emma's artwork in a frame.

Emma pointed to the picture. "That's me and you in front of our house."

"Yes, it is."

"Mrs. Fillmore said it was really good."

"It is, sweetie. I love it."

The colors were really bright and pretty. A big yellow star hung in the blue sky and they stood on green grass. To the left was a shadowy figure that Lacey couldn't make out.

"Who's that?" she asked Emma.

"That's Gabe at his house."

"Oh." Of course. Why hadn't Lacey figured that out? Gabe had been a big part of their lives. But not anymore. She wondered how long it would be before they stopped missing him.

Emma pointed to the star. "And that's Daddy, because he watches over us."

"It's beautiful and you did a wonderful job. I'm so proud of you." Lacey ran her fingers over the dark wood frame. "Where did you get the frame?"

"Gabe gave it to me. He took down all the pictures of his son. I told him I needed a frame for your gift and he gave me one."

Lacey wasn't going to scold her for asking for things because now wasn't the time.

"I'll hang it in my room so I can see it all the time."

Emma clapped her hands again. "Oh, boy!"

"You have a lot of gifts to open—you better get started."

Emma grabbed a package and ripped off the bow that Lacey had carefully made. A noise sounded on the roof and Emma jumped onto the sofa and curled into her.

"What's that, Lacey?"

"It must be the wind. Go ahead and finish opening your gift."

A loud stomping sounded from the roof, and Emma stayed glued to her.

That wasn't the wind. Lacey wasn't sure what to think. Weird things were happening. She waited for the sound to stop, but it only got louder. Someone was walking on the roof.

"I'll go see what's going on." She got up, and Emma held on to the back of Lacey's Christmas pajamas, not willing to let her get too far away. Lacey opened the front door and the wind blew it back, almost knocking her down. The pinecone wreath clattered against the door.

"What is it, Lacey?" Emma whispered into Lacey's back.

"I don't..." Her words trailed off as she spotted a kennel at her feet. Someone had left it at their front door. A small dog was inside. The porch light and Christmas lights were on, but Lacey couldn't see anyone.

Emma spotted the dog. "Look, Lacey. It's a puppy. A puppy!" Emma knelt down by the kennel. "There's a note on it. What does it say? I see my name."

Lacey bent down to investigate. What was going on?

"Read it, Lacey."

She tried to focus on the paper while keeping an eye on their front yard. "It says, 'To Emma from Santa... Claus.'" She read slowly because she wasn't believing what she was reading. "At the bottom it says the dog's name is Merry Christmas."

"That's what I would've named her, too. Can we get her out? She's so pretty."

"Let's see what's on the roof first."

Lacey stepped over the kennel and almost kicked an unwrapped box with a bow on it. Looking down, she saw it was a toaster. *A toaster!*

Emma saw it then. "Lacey, Santa left you a toaster. He knew what you needed. Santa knows everything."

Did he? She walked out into the yard to look around. Emma was right behind her. It was still pretty dark out and Lacey couldn't see much but a dark sky with the sun lazily rising to the east.

"Lacey, Lacey, look!" Emma pointed to the sky. "It's Santa. He was here. Daddy sent him." Emma waved with both arms. "Daddy, I love you. Bye, Santa."

Lacey looked down at her sister. "Sweetie…" She was going to say something, but for the life of her she couldn't find words to disappoint her sister. Maybe there were miracles in a child's imagination.

"It was Daddy, Lacey. He knew I was sad and he sent Santa so I would believe and be happy. I saw him."

"You saw Daddy?"

"Yeah, weren't you looking? He was right there on the roof and he went back to heaven."

Lacey knew she should say something, but she'd encouraged Emma to believe, and she had to go with what she had told her. She didn't have much time to analyze the situation as the Wilson family came running up her walk.

"What's going on, Lacey?" Sharon asked, huddled in her housecoat. "The boys say they saw Santa outside your house and on your roof."

"We did," Brad said. "He left something at your door and then he was on the roof and just disappeared."

"You saw Santa?" Lacey asked, thinking she had to be dreaming.

"Yes. Jimmy and I were looking out the window, waiting, and suddenly there he was."

Emma got in Brad's face. "Santa is real. You lied. You don't know nothin'."

Lacey placed her hands on Emma shoulders just in case she was planning to throw a punch.

Instead of answering Emma, Brad said, "Come on, Jimmy. We have to go home and wait for Santa to come to our house."

Sharon hurried after her boys, but her husband hung behind. "Did you pay for a Santa?"

"No. I have no idea what's going on."

"Weird." He took one long look at her in her Christmas pajamas and then he walked off, shaking his head.

"Come on, Lacey." Emma took her hand. "We have to tell Gabe."

"Emma, no." But Emma ran across the yard to Gabe's front door and pounded on it with her fist.

"Gabe, it's Emma. Open the door."

"Sweetie, Gabe went back to Austin. Remember?"

"No, he's here," Emma insisted, pounding harder on the door. "Gabe, open the door. It's me. Open the door! Open the door!"

Lacey took a deep breath and wrapped her arms around her waist. It was cold and they needed to go back to their house, but how was she going to make Emma understand?

"Sweetie, stop beating on the door. We have to go back to our house. You have a new puppy and we have to take care of her."

"No." Emma defied her and Lacey was at a loss for what to do next.

She squatted and turned Emma to face her. "We have to go to our house. It's cold and Gabe's not here."

"He has to be. I got everything I asked Santa for, so Gabe has to be here. I believed, Lacey, just like you told me. Right here." She poked at her chest. "Gabe has to be here."

"Sweetie—"

"No!" Emma turned back to the door and resumed pounding. She beat on the blasted door until Lacey thought she would scream. Finally, Emma sank to her knees, heartfelt sobs racking her little body, "Gabe, it's me."

Lacey couldn't stand it any longer. She gathered Emma into her arms and stood. Emma sobbed onto her shoulder. "No, Lacey."

"Sometimes we don't get everything we ask for. You got two amazing gifts. Let's go home and be grateful and take care of Merry Christmas."

Emma sobbed into Lacey's neck. Lacey turned and carefully made her way from the door. Since it was dark, she was careful where she stepped. A clicking sound stopped her. She swung around and saw Gabe standing in the doorway; a light behind him showcased him clearly in jeans and a black T-shirt. His hair was tousled and he wore his cowboy boots. She blinked. She was dreaming. She had to wake up.

Emma had heard the sound, too, and lifted her head. She jumped out of Lacey's arms and flew to Gabe. "You're here. I knew you were. Why didn't you open the door?"

Gabe squatted. "What's up, kiddo?"

Lacey could see and hear Gabe. This wasn't a dream. He was here…in his house. How long had he been here? And why had he been hiding from them?

Emma took Gabe's hand. "Come on, you have to see what Santa brought. He was here. I saw him on our roof. Can you believe that?"

"No."

"Come see." Emma tugged him farther into the yard,

giving him no choice but to follow. Lacey trailed after them, her mind a jumbled mess of confusion.

Gabe picked up the kennel and the toaster, and they went inside to the warm house. He helped Emma get the small dog out. It was a brown-and-white Jack Russell terrier mix. The dog ran around the living room, into the kitchen and down the hall to the bedrooms. Emma was right behind it, giggling.

Lacey encouraged Emma to come open her presents. Total pandemonium ensued as the little girl tore into the gifts. Now that Gabe was there she was all sparkly and happy. Lacey felt a little sparkle herself.

Gabe sat on the sofa and Lacey curled up beside him. There was a scratch on his face and several on his hands. A suspicion formed in her mind. It didn't take a Mensa member to figure out that Gabe had created a little magic of his own this Christmas.

After Emma had oohed and aahed over everything, she went over to Gabe. "Why did you come back?"

Lacey scooted a little closer. She definitely wanted to hear his answer.

"Because I wanted to spend Christmas with you and Lacey."

He was smooth; she'd give him that. He had a lot of questions to answer, but they could wait.

"'Cause you love us," Emma said.

Gabe's skin paled and Lacey came to his rescue. "Let's hurry and get dressed so you can ride your bicycle," she said to Emma. Her sister was off like a shot.

"I rather like what you have on," Gabe remarked.

She made a face at him as she walked out. She quickly changed into black slacks, a white pullover sweater and boots.

Gabe was sitting on the sofa when they came out.

Emma pointed to the box with the toaster in it. "Gabe, look what Santa brought Lacey. Now she won't burn toast anymore."

"That'll give the smoke alarm a rest," Gabe teased.

"Thank you," she mouthed, her eyes holding his for a moment. It wasn't a romantic gift. That would get too mushy, and they hadn't reached that level in their relationship. They never would now. So she would take the toaster and be happy.

GABE TOOK EMMA outside to help her ride the bicycle, and Lacey stayed behind to put a roast on for dinner. He didn't plan to stay, but he found himself lingering even though he knew he should go.

Emma mastered the bicycle in a few minutes and he sat on the curb and watched her ride back and forth. Soon Lacey joined him.

"Look, Lacey. Look at me," Emma shouted, Merry Christmas running behind her.

"I see you. You're doing good."

"Do I look cool?"

"Frosty."

There was silence for a moment, and then she looked at Gabe. "Why did you really come back?"

He wanted to say what she wanted to hear, but he couldn't. He went with the truth instead.

"I made it to Austin and rented a room in a hotel, called Dana and got something to eat. Later, I drove to a gas station and there was a little boy outside who was trying to find a home for the dog. I looked at it and thought Emma would love her and, before I knew it, I was driving back to Horseshoe. I bought the toaster on the way."

He rested his forearms on his knees. "I kept thinking how hard it was going to be for you with Emma not believing in Christmas. I just wanted to create a little magic."

"You did that. The Wilson boys saw you on the roof and are sure you were Santa. They now believe, too. And Emma even says she saw Daddy on the roof. You created a lot of magic."

"It was dark. How could they see me and mistake me for Santa Claus?"

"It's Christmas morning. Kids are looking for Santa, and when they see a shadowy figure on a roof they automatically think…ah, Santa."

"Mmm."

"From the scratches on your face and hands I take it climbing onto the roof wasn't so easy."

"I wanted to get your attention to come to the door, and the only way I could think to do that was to climb to the roof and stomp around. Cowboy boots did me in. I slid off into your bushes."

She suppressed a laugh. "How did you know she wanted a dog? She never told me."

"I just went by how much she loved Pepper."

"It's what she asked Santa for at the mall. So, as Santa, you're right on target, especially since you were here this morning. She also asked that you would always be in our lives, and she wanted to see Daddy one more time. Everything she asked for has come true, and now she believes more than ever. All because of you."

"Maybe there is something magical about Christmas, because I had no idea she wanted a puppy and I have no idea how she saw her dad on the roof. It was me."

"It was enough." Lacey laid her head on his shoulder. "You're wonderful. You made one little six-year-old very happy. I'm not too unhappy myself."

"I planned to quietly leave, but I heard Emma crying and I couldn't do it." He leaned his head against hers. "I still have to go, Lacey. I can't stay."

"You're staying for dinner," she said, as if he hadn't spoken. "No arguments."

He didn't argue. Lacey cooked a fabulous meal and they were finally able to drag Emma into the house. Merry Christmas rested at her feet. Emma chatted nonstop, which helped alleviate the tension between the adults. She was happy and that was what Gabe had wanted, but the sadness in Lacey's eyes tore at his heart.

After dinner, Emma fell asleep on the couch with the dog. He helped Lacey with the dishes. She was very quiet.

He leaned against the counter. "I guess I shouldn't have come back. It's too hard for both of us."

She wiped the counter and then turned to him. "Have you thought about what made you come back?"

"Lacey, I can't analyze it any further than I have. I have to go to find me. I don't know if I'm supposed to live in my other world or if I belong here. I have to make the right decision for all of us. Please, don't make this difficult."

She carefully laid the Frosty the Snowman dish towel on the counter. "I'll always be grateful for what you did today. But I can't go through another goodbye." She walked past him into the dining room. "Please say goodbye to Emma. She'll be disappointed if you don't."

"Lacey…" The pain in her voice ignited so many responses, but he had to ignore them. He couldn't stay and regret that decision later. He had to be sure of what he wanted, even though it seemed as though he was looking at everything he'd ever dreamed about.

She lifted her head and met his eyes. "Take care of

yourself, and don't let grief overtake you again." Her voice cracked on the last word and she walked out to the patio, quietly closing the door.

There was no need to go after her. They'd said everything they had to say. Now they just needed time.

Emma came in from the living room rubbing her eyes, her blond hair everywhere. Merry Christmas barked at her feet. He picked Emma up and sat her on the stool.

"It's time for me to go, kiddo. Take care of Lacey and Merry Christmas."

"I will. When are you coming back?"

His gut clenched. "I don't know." He hugged her and kissed her cheek. "Never stop believing."

"I won't. Bye, Gabe."

He walked out of the house, got in his truck and drove away. This time he knew it was for good. But he couldn't explain the feeling that everything he loved was in Horseshoe, Texas.

Lacey sat on the patio, tears rolling down her cheeks. She didn't want to cry, but she couldn't help herself. The wind stirred the fall leaves and blew them against the fence. They clung to a bare rose bush like ugly Christmas ornaments. Children's laughter sounded down the street. It was Christmas. Everyone was happy. Except her.

Emma crawled into her lap, facing her. "Don't cry, Lacey."

She drew in a deep breath. "I'm not crying."

With her forefinger, Emma touched Lacey's wet cheek. "You're weird, Lacey."

"Okay. Maybe a little," she admitted.

"Gabe'll come back."

"You think so, huh?"

"Yeah, because I believe in here." She jabbed at her

chest. "And you have to believe in there." She jabbed at Lacey's chest. "That's what you told me and it's true. All you have to do is believe."

Lacey smiled through her tears. "Do you know how much I love you?"

"Bunches."

"Oh, yeah. Bunches and bunches." She held her sister. She would believe until Gabe returned. That was all she could do. With belief, she had hope, and she would never let go of that. Not ever.

Chapter Eighteen

As Lacey went back into the house, the doorbell rang. She paused, wondering who that could be on Christmas Day.

"I'll get it," Emma said and ran to the door.

Lacey slowly followed.

"Who are you?" Emma asked.

Lacey pulled the door wider and froze. It was her mother, dressed to the nines in a stunning navy-and-white dress and to-die-for heels. Mervin stood behind her, holding a big package.

"Mom!"

Her mother was here.

"Hello, dear. I hope we're not intruding."

"No. No, please come in. I called you several times and you didn't answer."

"I had to do a lot of thinking," her mother replied.

Lacey pulled Emma to the side so they could enter.

"It smells good in here," Mervin said.

"I made a roast for lunch today. Would you like a piece of pie and coffee?"

"That's too much trouble." Her mother dismissed the offer with a wave of her hand. "We're on the way to spend Christmas with Mervin's daughter in Dallas."

"Is the pie homemade?" Mervin asked.

"Yes."

"Then that settles it," he decided. "We'd be happy to have coffee and pie. My daughter buys everything from the bakery."

"Mervin—"

"Joyce, relax and visit with your daughter."

Emma looked up at Joyce, evidently tired of being ignored, and asked, "Who are you?"

Her mother tried to look everywhere but at Emma. Eventually, she brought her gaze to the child. "I'm Lacey's mother."

"You're pretty."

Her mother blushed and the tired expression on her face vanished. "Thank you, dear." She took the package from Mervin and handed it to Emma. "We brought you something."

"Oh, boy! Thank you." Emma took the package and ran to the sofa to open it.

Lacey had never thought this day would come. Maybe her dad had been here that morning, because this certainly was a miracle.

Emma tore the paper away and Merry Christmas sniffed around her mother's feet.

"Oh, dear. A dog." Her mother was not that fond of dogs.

"That's Merry Christmas," Emma told her. "She won't hurt you. Look, Lacey." Emma opened a big wooden box full of pencils, crayons, markers and art paper. Emma jumped up and hugged Joyce around the waist. Joyce stiffened; even Lacey could see that. "Thank you. I love to draw. I draw real good." Emma went back to the box and Lacey's mother stood as if frozen in place.

Then, as if in slow motion, another miracle happened. Her mother removed her cashmere coat and laid it on the arm of the sofa. She sat on the sofa with the box between her and Emma.

"You look just like Lacey did when she was your age."

"I know," Emma replied. "Everybody tells us that."

Lacey hated to leave them alone, but everything was going so nicely that she didn't think her mother would do or say anything to hurt Emma. "I'll make coffee and serve pie."

"Okay, dear."

All Lacey could think was that her mother had come. She'd made the effort, and it was the best Christmas gift ever, except for seeing Gabe that morning.

"This pie is delicious," Mervin said.

"Thank you."

"Everything looks so nice, dear," her mother said as Lacey handed her a cup of coffee.

Lacey wanted to cry. She could feel the tears welling up at the back of her eyes. Her mother had praised her instead of criticizing.

The rest of the afternoon went the same way. Her mother talked more and more to Emma instead of over her head. When her mother mentioned that Lacey loved Barbies, Emma ran to her room to get hers, which totally shocked Lacey. Emma never played with the Barbies. But that afternoon Joyce and Emma sat on the sofa and dressed and redressed Barbies. It was a moment out of time.

All too soon, Mervin said it was time to go. Lacey felt a tug at her heart because she didn't want them to. She wanted to hang on to this moment when maybe... just maybe they had started to become a family.

Then Emma shocked her. "Can you be my grandma?" she asked Joyce.

Joyce clutched her chest. "Oh, dear. I'm too young to be a grandmother."

Mervin choked on his coffee. "Good one, Joyce."

He sat down by Emma. "You know, Emma, I have three grandchildren and they call me Pappy. If you need a grandpa, I'm your man."

"Oh, boy. I don't have a grandpa, either. You can be my…pappy." Emma giggled as she said the last word.

Her mother was now on the spot, and Lacey did nothing to help her. It would be a defining moment. Joyce played with the pearls around her neck and time stretched. Still, Lacey said nothing.

"Well, I guess, you can call me Jo… Nana."

Lacey hadn't even known she'd been holding her breath until air swooshed out of her lungs at her mother's reply.

"My friend Bailey calls her grandma nana."

"Then I'll be your nana."

Emma hugged Joyce, and Lacey saw tears in her mother's eyes. What a revelation. What a moment.

As they were leaving, Lacey hugged her mother and held on. She needed to. "Thank you," she said. "You've made me very happy. I love you."

It was a time in her life Lacey would never forget: The day her mother had finally accepted Emma as part of their family.

WHEN GABE MADE it back to Austin, he went to sleep and didn't wake up until the next morning. He thought of Lacey. He wanted to feel all the emotions Lacey was feeling, but his were twisted and shredded and he didn't know if he could ever make sense of them. Or if he could love her the way she wanted. That was the reason he was in Austin alone, and had never felt more lonely than he was today.

He met Dana at the attorney's office and signed the divorce papers. The attorney and Dana would go before a judge, who would sign off on the divorce decree, and that would be that. From there, they drove to the house they'd shared with their son. Gabe braced himself for the emotional impact, but was surprised when he didn't have the urge to run.

Going into Zack's room, though, was another matter. He found himself touching the yellow band on his wrist as if he could draw strength from Lacey. Even so, he didn't have that overwhelming, crippling feeling. He had tucked it away in a vault in his heart, just like Lacey had told him to.

The room was full of Zack's belongings, from his TV, video games and movies to the basketball hoop over the bathroom door to his baseball, his glove and his soccer ball. Everything that was Zack was in here. And there wasn't one thing Gabe wanted to keep. All his memories were stored in his heart, and that was all he needed, again just like Lacey had told him.

He and Dana agreed to donate all of Zack's belongings to a shelter so kids could enjoy them. Zack would like that. He told Dana she could have everything in the house. He wanted nothing except his clothes.

Before he left, he forced himself to walk to the spot where Zack had died. The bits and pieces of the four-wheeler were still there, scattered on the ground. He took a deep breath and said goodbye to all the pain and suffering. All he wanted now were peace and good memories of the child he'd loved. He was able to do that because of Lacey and her loving nature. As he made his way to his truck, the tangled mass of confusion inside him still raged on.

Over the weekend, he and Dana cleared out the house. They put the house on the market and, on Monday, Gabe went to the law firm to meet with the senior partner, Ted Silversteen. He was welcomed back with open arms. His old office was waiting for him and everything in it was just as he'd left it.

The next day he went to work and time slipped away as he got back into the routine of being an attorney. It was as if he'd never left. But a big part of him knew that he had. He also knew he was well on the way to full recovery.

The next week he rented a furnished one-bedroom apartment and moved in. He settled into his life in Austin. He was invited to dinners and parties by partners in the law firm. Inevitably, there was a single woman he just had to meet. He took all of this in stride because he knew they were trying to help him adjust. They just didn't know it was always the wrong woman.

THE DAYS PASSED quickly for Lacey. She stopped listening for the sound of Gabe's truck. The news of Santa visiting Emma had spread through Horseshoe quickly, and Emma told her story over and over to anyone who would listen. She now believed there was a Santa, and no one dared to tell her otherwise.

Lacey's mother had done a complete about-face concerning Emma. She called several times and came to visit before Emma's break ended. Lacey didn't question it. She just accepted the amazing gift.

With Emma back in school, the house was very quiet, and Lacey grew restless. She had to find something to do with her life. Emma was growing more and more independent. She had friends now and her aggressive behavior had stopped. She didn't even care if Lacey was late picking her up. All the anger she'd had inside was gone, and she didn't need Lacey as much.

Lacey wasn't sure what she could do in the small town, but then something fell into her lap. She was visiting with Angie at the bakery and discussing her plight when Angie mentioned that the woman who owned the flower shop two doors down was looking for someone to take it over. Lacey met with Mrs. Hinson, and after thinking about it for a couple of days, she bought the shop.

Her first order of business was to do a lot of redecorating. She painted and replaced the worn linoleum with big pink-and-white tile squares. The blinds were dingy, so she took them down and installed pink-and-white-striped shades. She bought two white wicker chairs and had the cushions covered in a pink-and-white stripe. The look was fresh and feminine.

She had looked at the previous owner's books, but she had no idea how busy she would be. It turned out she had two weddings the first week and there always seemed to be a special occasion that required flowers. The shop kept her running during the day. She loved working with flowers and decorating. She opened at nine and closed at two because she had to pick up Emma. If she had deliveries to make, she made them then. After that, it was Emma time.

Weeks turned into a month and then another. Still, she had no word from Gabe. As more time passed, she knew the likelihood of him returning was small. She kept believing, though.

At the end of February, Lacey helped Peyton give a baby shower for Angie. Lacey made the decorations extraspecial with pink, blue and white flowers. It was a fun day for everyone.

By mid-March Lacey had to face the fact that Gabe wasn't coming back. Even Emma had stopped asking. She still checked on Pepper's grave, but Lacey noticed she was doing it less frequently. Time had passed and his feelings had changed. Lacey had to accept that.

She just hoped he'd found peace.

GABE HAD WORKED LATE. The firm had represented a hospital in a lawsuit and they'd won. Two of the single lawyers in the firm invited him out to celebrate. Of course, such celebrations were always in a bar. Tonight the bar was on Sixth Street. The other two guys were dancing with women they'd met. Gabe sat at the bar with a woman named Sonya, who presumably was his date. She was blue-eyed and gorgeous.

"What would you like to drink?"

"Strawberry margarita" was her reply. It was hard to hear with all the chatter, laughter and the band playing in the corner.

Gabe signaled the bartender and made the order. He'd already ordered Scotch on the rocks for himself.

"What's that yellow band on your wrist?" she asked as the bartender placed the drink on a napkin in front of her.

He raised his wrist. "It keeps me sane."

She took a sip of the margarita, her eyes on him. "Are you known for going insane?"

"Regularly."

"I like a man who's not afraid to have fun."

He swirled the ice in his glass. This was where he was supposed to make his move and they would spend the night at her place or his. In that moment, he realized he wasn't in his twenties anymore and the parties and the late nights were just a way to get through the day in another way.

She pointed toward the entrance. "Your friends are leaving. I guess we should go, too."

Following her gaze, Gabe ran his finger over the yellow band and all the emotions that were tangled inside him suddenly began to unravel. He knew what he wanted. He wasn't confused. He wasn't blinded by grief. He wasn't going through the motions anymore.

Setting his glass on the bar, he replied, "Yes, it's time to go."

LACEY WAS HAVING a bad day. The flower delivery had been late and she'd had several arrangements to go to the funeral home. She got them there by twelve.

Emma's bows had gotten the attention of the mothers at school, and they'd asked if Lacey would make bows for their daughters. Now she had several to make by tomorrow. Right after she made an arrangement for the D.A.'s secretary. It was her birthday, and Hardy wanted the flowers delivered after lunch.

Who knew she would be so busy in this little town? But she'd found a home here with wonderful people in a place where she could raise Emma without the worries of the big city.

After finishing the arrangement, she ran across the street to the courthouse to deliver it and then hurried back. Merry whined, wanting to go to the bathroom. Lacey opened the shop's back door. There was a graveled parking area and a grassy verge. "Hurry, I have work to do."

Merry darted out at the same time the shop's front door bell jingled.

"I'll be right there," she called. "Come on, Merry,"

she said to the dog. Once Merry was back inside, Lacey hurried to the front. Nobody was there. She turned and saw a man sitting in one of the wicker chairs. She almost didn't recognize him. He wore jeans, a white shirt and boots. A Stetson lay in his lap.

Gabe!

What was he doing there?

He stood up with his hat in his hand. "You look good." He pointed with his hat. "Your hair's longer."

She touched it self-consciously. "Uh…yes, I'm letting it grow. I only cut it when my dad was so sick and I didn't have time to take care of it. The short style was easy." She was rambling because she didn't know what else to say. Her palms were sweaty and her nerves were tied up like a pretzel. It was just such a shock to see him.

"Can I get you a cup of coffee?" She moved toward the front counter.

"No, I've had more than enough for the day." He glanced around the shop. "Very nice. You found something to do that suits you."

"Yes." Lacey was so nervous she didn't know what to do with her hands, so she shoved them into the pockets of her smock. There had never been this kind of awkwardness between them. Now it was a viable thing she could feel. It was more about nerves and disappointment than anything else.

She raised her eyes to his and stared into his dark ones. For the first time she noticed that all the pain and disillusionment were gone. His eyes were clear and bright. The lines pain had etched on his face had also disappeared. He had finally put the tragedy behind him.

To calm her nerves, she rushed into a speech. "How are you? You look good, too. The city agrees with you."

"Could you please come out from behind the counter?"

"Uh…" She didn't want to. She wanted to postpone the heartache as long as possible. But she graciously walked around the counter to his side.

Merry sniffed at his feet.

"Hey, Merry Christmas." Gabe bent to rub the dog's head. Then he straightened and set his hat on the counter. "Aren't you curious why I'm here?"

She bit her lip. "Yes."

"I've finally found that peace I've been searching for."

"Oh…I'm happy for you." She wanted to reach out and touch him, but she kept her hands firmly in her pockets.

"When I left here, I was a man adrift and I didn't know if I could love again the way a man should. You deserve to be loved, Lacey."

She curled her hands into fists, bracing herself for what would come next.

"I've had a lot of time to think in the past few weeks, and I know now that I can have those feelings. I've had them all along, but the pain blocked them. The block was caused by guilt—guilt over my son's death. If he didn't have a life, then I didn't merit one, either."

Gabe raised his left wrist. "This yellow band has gotten me through the past weeks. As long as I could touch it, I could walk into my old home, even go through Zack's things without falling apart. I even went to the spot where he died. I did all these things with my hand on the yellow band. I dived into my work never realizing what this band meant to me, but now I do. I know exactly where I belong. I know exactly who I am and what I want in life." He cupped her face with the palm of his hand. "I can love you now the way a man should. Completely." He ran his thumb over her bottom lip. "Your lips aren't red."

A smile blossomed in her chest and rose up through her throat to her mouth. "They need to be. So badly."

He took her in his arms and his lips met hers with passion and power. The anguish of the past few weeks faded away as she tasted happiness once again.

"I love you," he whispered into her mouth. "I belong here with you and Emma. This is where I want to be for the rest of my life."

She rested her face against the warmth of his neck. "Are you sure?"

"Look into my eyes. What do you see?"

The smile rose up once again. "I see a man who has finally recovered from tragedy. I see us. I see a future."

He swung her around and sat in the chair with her on his lap. "I'm going to open a law practice here in Horseshoe. I always wanted to be a small-town lawyer." He tucked her hair behind her ear and she kissed his palm. "Will you share that life with me?"

"Yes, if I can bring a six-year-old along."

"I wouldn't have it any other way."

They sat there for a long time—her head on his shoulder, his arms around her waist as he told her about everything that had happened in Austin.

"When I was with that woman in the bar, I knew I didn't want to sleep with anyone but you. The crazy, lovely lady is the only one I want."

"I love you," she murmured. She touched his face, his throat, his hair. "I can't believe you're here. I've missed you so much, and Emma—" She jumped from his lap. "Oh, good heavens! I have to pick up Emma. She'll be so excited."

"Let's go, then."

"In a minute." She slid back onto his lap and wrapped

her arms around his waist, resting her head on his chest. "I just need to feel you a little while longer."

He kissed the side of her face. "I'm going to love you and Emma forever."

Forever would be just enough time.

Epilogue

Two weeks later...

Christmas was supposed to be the happiest time of the year, but for Lacey it would always be this April day when she stood at the back of the church in the designer gown her mother had insisted on and stared at Gabe in a tux at the altar, his dark eyes as warm as the love in her heart.

A ripple of excitement ran through her. Her fantasy had come true. She was marrying the man of her dreams.

Her mother and Mervin sat in the front row on the left, and the Wiznowski family and the rest of the town were gathered behind them. Angie and Hardy were at the end of the pew with their new baby son between them. The Rebel family took up the pews on the right and gave new meaning to the roguish-outlaw look. Lacey was getting used to Gabe's nephews and their charming appeal.

After the reception, she and Gabe were flying to Hawaii for a week. Her mother was staying with Emma. Lacey didn't worry because she knew Emma had formed a special connection with her new nana.

"The Power of Love" by Celine Dion filled the church. Emma looked up at Lacey. "Is it time to get married, Lacey?"

Emma looked like a doll in her white dress with a band of white miniature roses Lacey had made in her hair. "Yes, sweetie. It's time."

Emma stepped out with her basket in her hand and dropped rose pedals all the way to the altar.

How Lacey wished her dad could have been there to walk her down the aisle. She closed her eyes briefly and he was there, just as he'd been for the past several months.

The music stopped and "Here Comes the Bride" began. Lacey took one step, then another, her eyes on Gabe. Her breath caught as he came down the steps to meet her. After he lifted her veil, their eyes met and Lacey saw everything she'd ever wanted.

He took her arm and walked her the rest of the way to the priest. They would never be alone again. No more books in her head to consult or angst. Through all the heartache, pain and tragedy, they'd made it. The sun had burst forth through the darkness in a dazzling array of bright colors, and the future was theirs to reap. A future full of love, happiness and sharing.

All because they'd believed.

* * * * *

Look for Linda Warren's new miniseries,
TEXAS REBELS,
about Kate Rebel and her family,
coming soon only from
Harlequin American Romance!

#1529 A COWBOY OF HER OWN
The Cash Brothers • by Marin Thomas
Porter Cash has always been commitment shy—then he has a run-in with Wendy Chin, who makes the cowboy think about settling down. But her family obligations mean Porter is the *last* man Wendy can be with!

#1530 THE NEW COWBOY
Hitting Rocks Cowboys • by Rebecca Winters
Former navy SEAL Zane Lawson has come to the ranch land of Montana to find his peace. But he won't rest until he discovers Avery Bannock's secret—the one thing keeping them from being together.

#1531 TEXAS MOM
by Roz Denny Fox
Delaney Blair swore she was through with Dario Sanchez when he left her. But for the sake of her sick child, she goes to Argentina to tell Dario that he is needed by the son he never knew he had—and by Delaney!

#1532 MONTANA VET
Prosperity, Montana • by Ann Roth
In a stroke of luck, veterinarian Seth Pettit walked into Emily Miles's shelter at a critical time. But as the charming vet becomes indispensable, Emily wonders when her luck will run out...

REQUEST YOUR FREE BOOKS!
2 FREE NOVELS PLUS 2 FREE GIFTS!

HARLEQUIN

American ★ Romance

LOVE, HOME & HAPPINESS

YES! Please send me 2 FREE Harlequin® American Romance® novels and my 2 FREE gifts (gifts are worth about $10). After receiving them, if I don't wish to receive any more books, I can return the shipping statement marked "cancel." If I don't cancel, I will receive 4 brand-new novels every month and be billed just $4.74 per book in the U.S. or $5.24 per book in Canada. That's a savings of at least 14% off the cover price! It's quite a bargain! Shipping and handling is just 50¢ per book in the U.S. and 75¢ per book in Canada.* I understand that accepting the 2 free books and gifts places me under no obligation to buy anything. I can always return a shipment and cancel at any time. Even if I never buy another book, the two free books and gifts are mine to keep forever.

154/354 HDN F4YN

Name	(PLEASE PRINT)

Address	Apt. #

City	State/Prov.	Zip/Postal Code

Signature (if under 18, a parent or guardian must sign)

Mail to the **Harlequin® Reader Service:**
IN U.S.A.: P.O. Box 1867, Buffalo, NY 14240-1867
IN CANADA: P.O. Box 609, Fort Erie, Ontario L2A 5X3

Want to try two free books from another line?
Call 1-800-873-8635 or visit www.ReaderService.com.

* Terms and prices subject to change without notice. Prices do not include applicable taxes. Sales tax applicable in N.Y. Canadian residents will be charged applicable taxes. Offer not valid in Quebec. This offer is limited to one order per household. Not valid for current subscribers to Harlequin American Romance books. All orders subject to credit approval. Credit or debit balances in a customer's account(s) may be offset by any other outstanding balance owed by or to the customer. Please allow 4 to 6 weeks for delivery. Offer available while quantities last.

Your Privacy—The Harlequin® Reader Service is committed to protecting your privacy. Our Privacy Policy is available online at www.ReaderService.com or upon request from the Harlequin Reader Service.

We make a portion of our mailing list available to reputable third parties that offer products we believe may interest you. If you prefer that we not exchange your name with third parties, or if you wish to clarify or modify your communication preferences, please visit us at www.ReaderService.com/consumerchoice or write to us at Harlequin Reader Service Preference Service, P.O. Box 9062, Buffalo, NY 14269. Include your complete name and address.

HAR13R

Porter grew quiet for a minute then said, "One day I'm going to buy a ranch."

"Where?"

"I've got my eye on a place in the Fortuna Foothills."

"That's a nice area." Buying property in the foothills would require a large chunk of money, and she doubted a bank would loan it to him.

What if Porter was rustling bulls under Buddy's nose and selling them on the black market in order to finance his dream? As soon as the thought entered her mind, she pushed it away.

"So what do you say?" he said.

"What do I say about what?"

"Having a little fun before we pack it in for the night?"

"It's late. I'm not—"

"Ten o'clock isn't late." When she didn't comment, he said, "C'mon. Let your hair down."

"Are you insinuating that I'm no fun?" she teased, knowing that it was the truth.

"I'm not insinuating. I'm flat out saying it's so."

She'd show him she knew how to party. "Go ahead and stop somewhere."

Two miles later Porter pulled into the parking lot of a bar. When they entered the establishment, a wailing soprano voice threatened to wash them back outside. Karaoke night was in full swing.

"How about a game of darts?" Porter asked.

"I've never played before."

"I'll show you how to hit the bull's-eye." He laid a five-dollar bill on the bar and the bartender handed them two sets of darts. Then Porter stood behind Wendy, grasped her wrist and raised her arm.

"What are you doing?" she whispered, when his breath feathered across the back of her neck.

"Showing you how to throw." He pulled her arm back and then thrust it forward. She released the dart and it sailed across the room, hitting the wall next to the board.

"You're not a very good teacher," she said.

"I'm better at other things." The heat in his eyes stole her breath.

If you kiss him, you'll compromise your investigation.

Right now, she didn't care about her job. All she wanted was to feel Porter's mouth on hers.

He stepped back suddenly. "It's late. We'd better go."

Wendy followed, relieved one of them had come to their senses before it had been too late—she just wished it had been her and not Porter.

Look for A COWBOY OF HER OWN
by Marin Thomas, available January 2015
wherever Harlequin® American Romance®
books and ebooks are sold.

American Romance®

Homecoming Cowboy

Living on her grandfather's ranch, surrounded by her
loving brothers and their families, is helping
Avery Bannock put her painful past behind her.

After a decade undercover, Zane's ready to settle in
Montana horse country. Now he's got to convince the
gun-shy archaeologist that he's the only cowboy for her.
As they work together to find out who's stealing tribal
artifacts from a nearby reservation, Zane will do
everything in his power to win Avery's trust…and turn
their budding romance into a mission possible!

Look for
THE NEW COWBOY
by REBECCA WINTERS,

**available January 2015 wherever
Harlequin® American Romance®
books and ebooks are sold.**

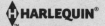

American Romance

What she needs

Emily Miles already has plenty on her plate. She has to care for the dogs she rescues, find staff and volunteers for her shelter, not to mention raise money to keep The Wagging Tail going. She can't jeopardize the shelter by getting involved with Seth Pettit.

Seth has his own plateful: a teenage ward who hates him, an estranged family he's trying to mend fences with and a living to make in small-town Montana. Tough but delicate Emily needs a full-time partner, and that just can't be him. Not as a vet *or* a man. So why does he want to be both?

Look for
MONTANA VET
by ANN ROTH

available January 2015 wherever Harlequin® American Romance® books and ebooks are sold.

HAR75553

HARLEQUIN®
A *Romance* FOR EVERY MOOD™

Love the Harlequin book you just read?

Your opinion matters.

Review this book on your favorite book site, review site, blog or your own social media properties and share your opinion with other readers!

Be sure to connect with us at:
Harlequin.com/Newsletters
Facebook.com/HarlequinBooks
Twitter.com/HarlequinBooks